MW01505166

Twice Around a
MARRIAGE

Twice Around a
MARRIAGE

by
Robert Olen Butler

TCU
Press

Fort Worth, Texas

Library of Congress Cataloging-in-Publication Data

Names: Butler, Robert Olen author
Title: Twice around a marriage / Robert Olen Butler.
Description: Fort Worth, Texas : TCU Press, 2025. | Includes
   bibliographical references.
Identifiers: LCCN 2025028892 | ISBN 9780875659381
Subjects: LCSH: Remarried people--Fiction | Older people--Fiction |
   COVID-19 Pandemic, 2020-2023--Fiction | Storytelling--Fiction | LCGFT:
   Novels
Classification: LCC PS3552.U8278 T95 2025 | DDC 813/.54--dc23/eng/20250715
LC record available at https://lccn.loc.gov/2025028892

Chapter opener illustrations by 3dcr3at3. © 3dcr3at3/Adobe Stock

TCU Box 298300
Fort Worth, Texas 76129
www.tcupress.com

In memory of my wife Clara Guzman Herrera.

She gifted everyone who came before her—friend or stranger—with her genuine and unmitigated love. The world is a poorer place without her.

Acknowledgements

My ardent thanks to Jeff Guinn, who has long known better than anyone how to read my work. Your regard has sustained me. And to Dan Williams and the TCU Press for providing a habitat for literary fiction in a tumultuous time. It is a joy to work with you.

March 18, 2020

That nascent spring in Paris in the time of the pandemic, on the first morning of the full French national lockdown, Howard and Amanda step from their Airbnb bedroom and onto their eighth-floor balcony. Still in their modestly unisex sleeping clothes, shoulders not quite touching, they lean into the railing and ignore the Paris skyline, instead focusing on the sixty acres of the Parc des Buttes-Chaumont splayed before them.

Amanda says, "Well, if we must. There it is."

"Yes," Howard says. *"In Search of Lost Time."*

These are the first words they have exchanged since arising a few minutes ago, but each of them knows what the other is saying.

Amanda: "Well, if we must be stranded on this six-hundred-square-foot island in the sky, at least we can look down upon the park where first we met half a century ago."

Howard: "Yes. Proust would have appreciated the unremitting confinement of these two rooms for such a search."

And having understood each other, they say no more.

Amanda slides now into a space in her brain like an athlete in the *zone*, a space that is—she would argue—far from the library cubicles where dwell Howard's brain and the brains of his scholarly ilk. She lives in the sunlit village square of her sense-driven imagination, where the scholarly modes of abstracting, explicating thought are forbidden.

She is a novelist. Of a literary sort.

So she gives herself over to the undulant seascape of treetops in the park before her. Linden and horse chestnut, honey locust and alder, beech and cedar. And off to the left, rising above all the others, a California sequoia. She knows the tree well. Fifty-two years ago she stood as close to it as she could get and yet see it whole. This she did an hour or so before there ever was a Howard, the thought of whom now shifts her gaze across the treetops to a visible fragment of a lake and a rocky rise to a faux Roman belvedere, the Temple de la Sybille.

This is where Amanda Duval and Howard Blevins first met, encircled by eight Corinthian columns and, beyond them, the rooftops of Paris. And from Amanda's zone, where it is now 1968, she sees him glance at her from near the circular stone bench beneath the domed roof. He looks away at once, but they each know what the other is doing. She moves toward the bench, and as she nears him, he casually turns to face her. As if: Oh yes, I've been expecting you. His hair is cut in a thick, shoulder-length shag. Hers is cut short. They are both charmed by the gender reversal. His face is clean-shaven, in deference, no doubt, to the deep cleft of his alluringly squared chin. She sees that he sees her seeing his chin. And so her first words ever to this man who will twice become her husband are, "A wise sartorial decision." And his first words to her are, "I love a close reader."

Shortly after, they stand beside each other and look toward the one hill of Paris taller than the Buttes-Chaumont: the distant Butte Montmartre, crowned with the domes and spires and bell tower of Sacré-Coeur.

She expects at least a flicker now of another moment-to-moment scene between the two of them. Talking with each other. Being with each other. But Amanda and her husband-to-be in 1968 have dissipated in her head into simply a neutral thought. A summarized passing of time. She fails to summon, for instance, fails even to imagine, whether their shoulders were touching. Or were not quite touching.

Meanwhile, Howard, standing beside her, outwardly surveys the same trees, the same lake and promontory, the same canopied columns where he met Amanda. But his zone is full of history and theme and motif and summaries.

He is a scholar. Of modernist literature. This city has always fed his mind.

He is pondering from the balcony how we have no alternative but to expect things to change. This hilltop—this present dense amassment of fifty species of trees stitched tight by five miles of roads and paths, a refuge where city dwellers can stroll and loll and sun—was once a prime Paris hanging ground and gibbet site, the latter centered around an infamous structure of sixteen pillars joined by three levels of transverse beams, a Paris proto-high-rise to accommodate five dozen lately hanged bodies

3

awaiting mass burial. And then this park became the slaughter ground for the daily deaths and retirements among the city's fifty thousand working horses. Slaughter and deconstruction, the knackers going after hides and hooves but then leaving the rest in mounds for the legion of Chaumont rats and for the weekly trench-dumping of whatever was left. Howard feels no imperative to render any of this as a scene in his head. Instead, he thinks, *The strolling and lolling and sunning that have in this latter day come to this place are as deceptively progressive as the time of Parisian drinking and lovemaking and creating that followed the Great War. It will not last. All things will change. And change again. As in this new plague that has begun to pass through.*

Howard and Amanda wordlessly turn to each other.

He shrugs.

She nods.

They retreat to the bedroom to prepare for the day. Given why they are in Paris—to go on together or not to go on—he finds himself surprisingly, if not incongruously, attuned to the flash of eyes as she turns. Her eyes are impervious to her age: pop-fashionably large, even for this era, but also redolent somehow—if only by his knowing who she is—of the books and books and books they have read. But her eyes have vanished and her back is to him on the other side of the bedroom. This gesture itself—its being her way since they remarried a decade ago—has registered within Howard as a wearily familiar regret, for he does enjoy seeing even flashes of her body. Though they have both turned seventy-two in recent months, she is something quite like beautiful to him still. Simply in a transformed way. He mulls this thought: *She's like the aging of a first edition of a modernist novel, its dust jacket lavish-seeming now in its deco geometry, its paper tinted like old ivory, and if you put your face into the middle of its pages, they have acquired over the years a faintly sweet smell, like vanilla.*

4

But Howard's metaphorizing does not lead him to a clarified thereness regarding Amanda's body. He simply rematerializes in the bedroom on the eighth floor of the apartment building on Rue Botzaris in the nineteenth arrondissement of Paris in the early twenties of this new century.

He is holding a shoe.

Before him the room is empty.

Amanda has finished dressing and is gone.

He hears the clank of a cooking implement from the far end of the apartment. She is commencing breakfast. How long has it been since she has done that for the two of them?

Now Amanda is watching Howard across their dining table next to the apartment's open-plan kitchen. He has taken a half piece of toast and is carefully dabbing up the remaining spilled egg yolk from the sunny-side-ups. He is savoring the very last of these bites, his eyes closed in gustatory bliss.

She responds to his face as she sometimes still does, when they aren't filling the space between them with a fog of words. She considers his chin, which she has always admired, a chin still as substantial in its angles as a Heritage Press *War and Peace* on a bedside table.

And his eyes open.

Though they are to her handsomely wide-set and the color of her morning dark-roast, they also remind her of that fog, as far too often they appear to be looking, to be seeing, but in fact they are turned inward to think and think and think.

As now he thinks he understands her gaze. "How long has it been?" he asks.

"Which *it* is that?" she says.

"Breakfast together without a café involved."

"Long enough for me to forget that habit of yours." She nods at his plate.

5

"With the toast?"

"The mopping. Yes."

"It's the denouement," he says.

"But of a modernist sort," she says. "A cold comfort of a climax, the deferred yolk."

"When was the last time you offered warm concluding comfort in your own work?"

"Ah," she says, choosing simply to concede the point. Never.

"Or any comfort for that matter," he says.

"I was not criticizing your beloved modernists," she says. "Or even your breakfast habits."

"Nor I your novels. Indeed, it's one of the things I admire in you. Your merciless gaze."

Amanda shrugs at this. She sips her coffee.

Howard sips too, lets their silence go on for a time. Then he says, "Breakfast together seems to have done us some good."

"What good, exactly?"

"We've been hovering."

"Over an argument."

"Yes."

"Anything in particular?" she asks, leaning slightly toward him and in a tone as if she's expecting him to introduce something on his mind that she—as is often the case—cannot predict. She's ready for that.

"No," he says. "As yet undetermined. But the point is that we neither of us have pounced."

"You credit the breakfast?"

"I do."

"The egg discussion in particular?"

"I believe so," he says.

"So *you're* taking credit," she says. "You and your toast."

"I am. We are."

Howard and Amanda look at each other for a moment, simultaneously aware of how adept they are at bickering. Sometimes dangerously. But sometimes adept, as well, at sliding away from genuine strife.

And so Amanda raises her coffee cup to him. "Then I drink to you."

He raises his.

She appends: "With a faintly dreggish last sip of room-temperature coffee."

"We make do with what we have left," he says.

They each think to add: *That's the story of our marriage.*

But neither does.

Both times, they further append to themselves. Married once for twenty-two years. And then, after a ten-year hiatus, a second time for nine and counting.

They clink. They drink.

Howard says, "This is going to be difficult. The lockdown."

"Yes," she says. "At least our Airbnb hosts seemed to know what was coming. They stocked the cabinets and fridge for a week or so."

"How are *we* stocked?" he says. "For work. I didn't expect to do much. Two weeks off. Not close work. But at the last minute I gave in to habit and brought my laptop. Did you possibly?"

Amanda did bring her laptop, also at the last minute, impulsively, for she'd finished her latest novel little more than a month ago. But yes. She has it.

"Yes," she says. "I have it."

"Thank *god,*" he says.

"Capital *G,*" she says.

They are being realistic in their relief. They are trapped inescapably together in six hundred square feet for at least two weeks and likely longer. Perhaps much longer. She may not have a book

7

to write, but she has a screen to stare at in a separated space for much of each day. And so does he. Which may somehow make their enforced togetherness manageable. And perhaps it will help them forego a sad irony: She and Howard came to Paris in large part to remind themselves of all the benign things they once were to each other; now Paris has set them up to be at their worst.

She plumps a forefinger on the dining tabletop. "Is this yours, then? For work?"

Howard says, "Is that okay?"

"I will write upon the bed," Amanda says.

"You and Proust."

"Me and Wharton."

"You and Joyce."

"He wrote lying on his stomach, in crayon," she says. "I'll stick with Wharton."

"Have it your way," he says.

"Get everything you need from the bedroom now, and I'll clear the dishes."

He has a flicker of hesitation.

She sees it.

He sees that she sees it and he says, "I know you'll be writing late. We both will. Rightly. Does everything I need include …"

"Not your jammies, baby boy. If it's time for you to sleep and I'm still going, I'll just take over your table."

"Deal." He has exhaled the word in relief.

They move to do what they've just contracted to do, but they each have an instant chill of a doubt that they are capable of pulling this off. From a creative point of view. Each happens to think, *We're whistling past the graveyard*, Amanda tolerant of the cliché because she is neither speaking nor writing it, Howard tolerant because he can footnote it as originating in a long poem titled "The Grave" written by a Scottish cleric named Robert Blair and published in 1743.

Shortly thereafter, Amanda closes the bedroom door behind her.

The beds are twin.

She retrieves her MacBook from her carry-on, takes off her ballet flats, and props herself up on her bed.

She nods at her bare feet whose toes flutter in response, this being a small ritual in any writing situation where her toes are visible, a ritual known to no one but herself. Amanda likes her feet after all these years, those toes still sweetly shaped, though they are happier now only with a somewhat wider shoe.

She opens her computer.

And she is instantly stymied.

Another work ritual has her linger upon the rocky brow and snout of Catalina Island—her computer's default wallpaper—until she has in her head the first few words, however tentative, of the day's writing.

But of course today there are no words.

There is no book.

She shifts her gaze to the French doors that open onto the balcony. Amanda herself closed them after she and Howard returned to the bedroom to dress for the day.

She gently folds her MacBook shut and puts it aside on the bed.

She rises and opens the doors and steps onto the balcony once again.

It is midmorning on a Tuesday. Rue Botzaris beneath her is empty. All the paths she can see among the trees in the Buttes-Chaumont are empty.

The city is silent.

The global virus is passing through.

And something stirs in her.

She has always scorned the drawing of inspiration from what other writers have done. But Camus and García Marquéz and Defoe and, yes, Boccaccio bump into her, drinks in hand, at this little party where she finds herself in her head. They bump and excuse themselves and pass on. Which is fine with her. She knows why these guys are here—each with his own literary plague—but she doesn't need other writers for her to sip the cocktail in her hand while dressed in her little black dress of inspiration. Maybe it would be all right to exchange a few words with Boccaccio. He began it all. Storytelling in the midst of the Black Death. And she would make it new. But she does not pursue him.

She realizes she may actually have work to do.

She returns to the bed.

And she flies away from Catalina Island to the Isle of Wordformac, where the world exists in working drafts.

She begins.

In the twenty-first year of the twenty-first century, in the spring of the coronavirus and on the first morning of the French lockdown, a man and a woman

Amanda stops.

She has arrived at this moment abruptly, as she always does, having begun a new book without initial conscious planning, expecting things to make themselves clear. After all, fiction is about identity, she knew. As an abiding creed. Every great novel is about the central characters engaging the eternal question: Who the fuck am I? And awaiting her characters now are the universal markers of identity. Names.

She looks toward the balcony, where she sees the two of them. They are in their early seventies. Leaning there.

She understands who they are.

Megan and Philip.

Validated by having fictional names for which Amanda has no personal associations.

All right then. She bends to her keyboard. She deletes their anonymity and continues with her opening sentence.

Megan and Philip step from their bedroom and onto their eighth-floor balcony. They stand beside each other, a small but intentional gap between them, and they look down upon the Parc des Buttes-Chaumont.

And now Amanda's hands pause and once again draw back from the keyboard, while her characters wait for her. She has done this often enough—for seven novels—so that an abrupt, blank-brained shutdown after writing the first few dozen words no longer alarms her. Even after she knows her characters' names. It is part of the process. It feels as if suddenly there is nothing before her, but she always senses—always believes—the opposite is true. An abundance is there, all of it asking to be next.

And the abundance in this moment feels legit.

Megan and Philip. Amanda and Howard.

In lockdown. In lockdown.

All of them locked down and opened up.

Amanda's hands deadfall to her lap. A gesture that accompanies a thought the like of which is forbidden in her creative zone:

The kernel of this novel's inspiration is presently being visited throughout the world upon all my fellow writers, glisteningly so, and even providing its own enforced writing time. And when we simultaneously deliver our manuscripts, all the literary agents and publishers in the world will quickly grow feverish with despair: "No," they will actually weep. "Please. No more."

"Fuck," Amanda says. Loudly.

Meanwhile, in the next room, Howard is prepping for an article-cum-chapter-cum-book intended to resurrect an underappreciated early Twenties modernist. The big project for his current sabbatical from his longtime academic home at Northwestern. A few years ago a small-printing, post-Great War novel that was long thought to be utterly lost came to Howard from a rare book dealer friend. A book set in wartime Paris before the Americans got involved, with an American journalist turned Secret Service agent as the central character. Stylistically the book had its own budding modernism in ways akin to what would later become associated with Hemingway. It also had the intriguing scent of a far-future literary movement, postmodernism: The writer published the book under a pseudonym but used his own real name—Christopher Cobb—for the central character, who, as far as Howard has been able to discover, was the author in far more than name. As for the rest of Cobb's career, he explored modernism mostly through flash fiction—at that time exclusively called short short stories—a form rare in that era outside of the mass market magazines. But Cobb worked hard at wresting the form from the commercial clutches of *Collier's* and *Cosmopolitan*, and his work appeared with some regularity in the modernist literary journals from *transition* to *The Little Review*, from *Pagany* to *Morada*.

All of this, in overview, shaped Howard's debut examination of Cobb for the academic community in the winter issue of the estimable *Journal of Modernism Studies*. Now it's time to write about Cobb in a nice, tight, close read of an article. Howard has chosen a Cobb work of flash fiction from *transition*. "Outside the Dingo."

From his chair at the table he has been staring for a time across the living room floor and out the French doors. But he is in focused concentration and so is seeing nothing. He is turning over words for a title, for a point of entry. And now at last they come to him in a rush: "Limning Cobb, a Tale of Two Commas."

"Ha," he says.

And he squares around to his computer screen to read Cobb's story one more time, fully armed:

what a nice bee-buzz is going on in my ears like a wide green field with plenty of flowers and bees not that I think much of flowers to be perfectly honest but it's nice to know there's flowers and me standing on some dirt road somewhere when I once was young and I even had my teeth and there's a field before me and all those things that in principle you like to see in a field and why not since I've just enough of the good stuff in me to be happy where I am in the dark on the Bowery under the Third Avenue El and happy where I once was and if those two places are far far apart then that's how life goes and I have some friends though I can't see them right now they're out on the mooch but for tonight I'm not as well because I found a few bucks inside a dead man's coat at least I think he was dead and if he wasn't he's a lucky man not to be and he's got my prayers with him forever and if I once had more than bottle-gang friends if I once had children and still do somewhere then that's how life goes and they're like teeth, children, useful when you got them but if you don't got them any more you can at least drink

And then a sound. A word.

Howard hears it, flinches at it.

He pauses and consciously composes a full, comprehending assessment but does not speak it, instead writing its words in his head: *"Fuck" I hear, quite clearly, in the voice of my wife through the closed door of the bedroom where she is doing her work but apparently with a dif-*

ficulty I devoutly hope is not contagious seeing as I am presently moving into a flow state in my own work.

This being a sentence, he is aware, composed with its own tale of two commas: a *quite clearly* audible *fuck* indeed, the descriptor emphatically and independently and exclusively and climactically comma-encased to express his acute irritation. All prompted by the word exclaimed by his wife, with whom he must share this cramped workspace during a parlous and likely extended time.

He doesn't blame her. She works in the way she must work. But the two of them have long known how to isolate themselves out of *Fuck!* range back home in Evanston.

Yet here we are, he thinks. *What are we to do?*

There are, however, for the moment, no further outbursts from the bedroom, so Howard brings up a blank page before him on his laptop and begins his process, as always, with a period of brainstorming, which may last a few days.

His word processing font is an old-style typewriter font from the 1960s, a Smith Corona Galaxie, Howard's own machine from high school through college, with an accompanying Apple audio application. He types:

>*Dingo Bar, Cobb & Hemingway*
>*Rush of first-person consciousness*
>*Molly Bloom voice*

And he pauses. He must begin to address the commas, which he is convinced are at the center of Cobb's story.

His hands go up, hang above the keyboard. And then:

>*The commas around children, the lingering that surrounds them after the rush of words, speaks of a felt loss, more than teeth*

14

>*Speaks also of his alcoholism. A drunkenly thoughtful pause. Speaks thus of his own children?*

And Howard continues on. With Amanda well aware of what he is doing, even through the closed door, because the Apple application turns his laptop keystrokes into a full-throated reproduction of the sound of a manual typewriter's keyboard. He has used this app for a long while, but it's been a little more than a long while since Amanda was within hearing range of him working.

"Holy Mary, mother of silence," Amanda beseeches aloud, though she believes moderately enough that her words will remain in the room with her.

But the clacking of the faux manual typewriter immediately ceases.

Her vehemence has bullhorned her.

A new *fuck* blooms in her head, but goes unvoiced.

The silence persists from the next room.

She suspects what's going on. And she suspects he suspects her suspicion, which makes it her move. She could play him by silently staying put. But she does not have the patience, which he knows and is presently exploiting.

She rises.

She goes to the door.

She waits, turning her head slightly, focusing her ear on the other side. She'd rather hear him breathing before she acts, to verify his readiness for a confrontation. She does not want to open the door and have him sitting across the room, before his computer, pretending simply to be thinking.

She places her ear on the door.

She believes she hears—faintly—the slip of his breath.

Just there.

All right.

She gently grasps the doorknob, readies herself, then turns the knob sharply and yanks open the door while simultaneously saying, "Do we need to talk?"

He is standing before her, as expected.

Her face and posture say, *This doesn't surprise me.*

While his face and posture say, *Your lack of surprise does not surprise me. Yes we need to talk.*

And he begins. "It's been a while, hasn't it."

"Since we've tried to work within earshot of each other?"

"Just so."

"It has been a while," she says.

"Remind me," he says. "Are intense verbal outbursts a necessary part of your process? They are extremely distracting."

"Are you referring to the recent *Fuck?*"

"I am."

Amanda hums a brief *hmm* while turning her face away, as if carefully considering his question. But the gesture is intentionally phony, a simple setup, and she quickly returns to him and rivets his gaze and says, "Yes. An occasional declaration of *fuck* is a necessary part of my creative process. But I must caution you that so is an occasional *fuck fuck fuckity fuck.*"

Howard shrugs. "Which is merely an egregious redundancy, it seems to me."

"Of course it seems so to you," Amanda says. "The repetition is actually a precise expression of emotion. You only know how to express ideas."

"That is my métier. Which does not require bellowing, no matter how emotionally expressive."

"But it does require the clacking cacophony of a simulated antique."

Howard cocks his head in dramatized puzzlement.

She says, "What do you have? An app that makes your laptop sound like a what? Your Papa's thirty-pound Underwood?"

"No."

He has said this in a voice small enough that it sounds almost vulnerable to Amanda. To his surprise, it sounds that way to Howard as well.

In that same tone he says, "Closer to the sound of my own first typewriter, a Smith and Corona Galaxie Twelve portable."

Which stops the conversation for a breath or two, as Amanda and Howard decide if or how to resume their snark.

"That sound is distracting as well," Amanda says, but gently.

"It's a precise expression of emotion as well," Howard says, with equal gentleness.

They breathe a bit more, softly.

Then Amanda says, "We hadn't planned on working anyway."

"But the lockdown," Howard says.

"Ah yes."

"Perhaps in shifts."

"Aren't we both first-thing writers?"

Howard grunts in assent.

"Are you flexible?" she asks.

"Only with great difficulty."

"Would you expect me to be?"

"No."

"You're right," she says.

"And the work must be daily," he says. "Once begun."

"And given the circumstances," she says. "The sessions are likely to run deep into the day."

"Even, if need be, into the evening."

They pause, and both become acutely aware that, for this consequential conversation, they are standing in a doorway between a small bedroom that faces, a few steps away, the door to a small bathroom and aware as well that this doorway is the only one within the apartment whose primary purpose is not to mask clothes hangers or pots and pans or poo.

Amanda says, "So do you wish to return to your work now?"

"Not if I can't rely on its being sustainable tomorrow and tomorrow and tomorrow."

"Because I might curse from behind this door, now and then?"

"And because you can't bear the sound of a classic typewriter."

Amanda thinks to somehow extract and weaponize the *petty* from the Macbeth quote Howard has invoked with his pretentious tomorrows.

But she does not. It's time to stop the salad-knife slash of their surface banter. The two of them have some serious problem-solving to do.

She shrugs off his last remark, literally sidesteps him, and moves into the living area. The balcony and the treetops beyond beckon, but she has stepped away from the bedroom in order to engage him, not distance him.

She stops, turns.

He has already emerged to face her.

She says, "Our discomfort runs way deeper than a little sound pollution. For our professional work the problem is simply *thereness*. I'm afraid we need solitude, Howard."

He nods, and he makes a little puckering gesture with his mouth.

Which he becomes instantly aware of, with regret.

He feels ready to do his part to stop all the little cuts they've been exchanging. "Sorry," he says. "That was not a snarky moue. Just a thoughtful pursing."

"Good to know," Amanda says.

"You're right," he says. "About our real challenge here."

"Thank you," she says. "I'm going to turn my back on you now. But it's only to find some fresh air."

"I understand."

So she turns her back and moves off toward the French doors and the balcony.

Howard returns to the dining table and sits before his computer. He reads over the dozen brainstorming points he recorded before his work time was expletively interrupted. As for that, he thinks, *So be it. She and her process are who they are, perhaps fuckities and all.*

He saves the notes and closes the laptop lid.

With a sigh. *Yes, she's right. About the solitude.* And his twice having felt moved to admit she's right, within a very few minutes, further moves him to offer mitigation to himself: *Once one simply has the spark for it, it's so much easier to do the sort of work that she does rather than engage in the rigors and the relinquishment of self that attend great scholarship.*

But then from a twinge of guilt he doubles back to the *spark* part to pay his wife her due: *She's a fine writer. It's a serious gift. There is rigor, too, in accessing that gift, manifesting it.*

And now that this little dialog has begun within him, the you-can-be-more voice replies with a not infrequent point: *Howard, you could do what she does. To some admirable—even publishable—degree, you could do what they all do, all these others that you've spent your life explaining to the world.*

"Yes," he replies, aloud. But his stay-in-your-already-superior-lane voice is growing irritable and asks, *Do you really believe that? Do you even care?* And Howard answers both questions, also aloud. "Yes." And "Yes."

"Yes yes yes what?" This is Amanda's voice, approaching.

Howard looks to her as she crosses the living room floor, the French doors open behind her.

He lies, "As in Molly Bloom saying yes and yes and yes. She simply appeared in some article notes I've put aside till the plague has passed."

"I've just had a thought about that," Amanda says, stopping

still. "About the plague passing by. This morning I thought of writers who've used wide contagion as a premise in their work, and one of those boys sidled up to me a second time, just now, while I was on the balcony."

Amanda pauses.

Howard makes a bit of a show peeking around her toward the balcony. "Has he gone?"

"Likely. But he left me with an idea."

"Monsieur Camus, no doubt?"

"Not Camus."

"It's his city."

"Not Camus."

"I've got a couple of aesthetic bones to pick with him."

"Hush now, Howard. Time to focus."

"You're the one who introduced the sidling boys of epidemic literature."

"I did. For a reason. But it's not about any of your modernists."

This hushes Howard. He suddenly thinks he knows who she has in mind.

"Consider Signore Boccaccio's *Decameron*," she says. "And his full-blown, Black Death pandemic. Those ten young people who've isolated themselves, hiding from it, telling each other tales to pass the time."

He was right.

But the next part will surprise him.

She prepares for it by placing the other dining table chair before him.

He picks up the cue and squares around to face her.

She sits and says, "The tales never mention the plague, but as diversely oblivious as they seem to be, you can see Boccaccio's throughline in them. Down in the subtext of it all is a quest to answer some questions relevant to you and me here in the midst of this plague. Who the hell have we been with each other? Has that worked? How do people live together? So let's write tales to tell each other, you and I. *Stories.* One each night, alternating. That gives us time to work on them and it gives us work to fill our time. We came to Paris to revisit the life you and I found together, to visit our *selves.* So let's make each story about that life we've lived. Together and apart. Any of it. Let's just write as truly as we can. But not as my ilk understands truth, that to get at it deeply you make it up. Just not for this. Not now. Not in this city. No true lies of literature. I hereby relinquish my artistic license."

She pauses.

She is puzzled. Howard had been nodding minutely along at her proposition until she reached her disavowal of the privileges of fictionists. His change was to an unreadable stillness, when she expected relief at her shifting the form closer to his own.

In fact, behind his silence was restrained disappointment. He'd been pleased at what was sounding like a chance to challenge her at her own game. Though he recognizes the sense of her suggestion, given the circumstances.

He does say, "But with the shape and pace and voice and feel of fiction, yes?"

"Yes," she says. "Yes. Absolutely. The personal essay form of so-called creative nonfiction. Creative in technique and focus but not in content. And here's what makes it work in these rooms we're stuck in: Though it will be in real story form, we'll also be creating a casual quasi-memoir, a reminiscence, so it will all be simply for ourselves, outside of our genres, with no eye to publication. We're just trying to get through a plague. So to hell with our professional writing process. Even if I occasionally curse and you pound away at your boyhood Smith Corona, it won't be a problem for these tales. Nor will they require absolute solitude.

An awareness of each other in the next room might actually be helpful in writing about our shared life."

Amanda stops speaking. She finds herself a bit breathless, for what she intended as a thoughtfully considered recommendation has come out as a flurry of impassioned advocacy.

She just wants to be able to write her way through all this.

Howard does not respond instantly.

Which is too slow for her, she discovers.

"What do you *say?*" She adds, pressing him so he will understand that if he says *no*, any further awkwardness between them during the lockdown will be his fault.

Howard takes himself in hand. His silence has come from choosing his words carefully, given his recent thoughts about his covert literary skills. He realizes he can still take her on at her own game. But he will keep that to himself. He makes it simple: "I say yes." Though he does add, "Perhaps I have an undiscovered knack."

Amanda says, "Perhaps it will drive you out of your mind. And I mean that in the best possible way."

Howard smiles. He leans forward and squeezes her hand.

March 19, 2020

By an hour after midnight Amanda has written a thousand good words. She now senses what needs yet to be done and how long she will need to do it. She can finish by reading time this evening. She closes her computer, slips it onto a lower shelf of the night table.

She rises into the space between their twin beds. Though it is narrower than the stretch of her arm, she is suddenly aware of the gap. She shouldn't find this odd. After all, though at home she and Howard still sleep in the same bed, its king size has for some time been separately inhabited, with a distinct no-one's zone of mattress between the two of them. It is an accommodation that has evolved almost unnoticed over these past couple of years.

But this formalization of the space between them makes her pause. Not that twin beds were a conscious choice in the booking. This is a bland little apartment they have chosen, outfitted from Tati and Carrefour. They simply wanted a balcony view of where they met, with no consideration of the owner's quotidian taste.

Still, here she stands, snagged. She thinks, *What the fuck?* Then: *Ah. The fuck is: I've had a long writing day with more than a soupçon of jet lag.*

She wills herself onward, approaches the bedroom door and opens it gently, so as not to disturb Howard in his own writing.

She hears no current keystrokes. Realizes, indeed, that she has not heard those distant faux typewriter sounds for a long while, though she cannot say for how long, as they soon became unnoticeable, a writerly white noise.

She intends to cross to the bathroom without even looking in his direction.

But with her first step Howard says, "Are you finished for the night?"

She stops and looks to him.

Across the way, at the dining table, his laptop is open and the screen shines brightly upon the side of his turned face.

"I am," she says. "And you?"

He looks at the screen.

He does not answer at once.

"I haven't heard your college portable," she says.

"The writing goes slowly, I suppose." And then he turns back to her. "I also turned off the clickity clack."

"Why? I didn't mean to …"

He stops her with the flash of his palm. "I realize," he says. "But you need to be out of your mind to write a story, didn't you say? And the sound would have kept you in your mind, stewing."

He's right. Amanda does not know whether to take his gesture as sensitive or snarky. For now, she nods a small, eyes-closed thanks.

Howard thinks: *It was keeping me in my mind, as well. My scholarly writing groove.* But he does not speak it: He silenced the Smith-Corona font purely for her sake even before he discovered the benefit to himself; it was intended for her, not for him.

"I need to shower," she says.

"I'm nearly done for the night," he says.

She steps into the bathroom, where she begins to undress, wishing she thought to bring her pajamas in with her.

When she is naked and about to step into the alcove shower, her eyes fall to the basin. Howard's wedding ring is there, beside the soap dish. Removed at some point to wash and dry his hands. She knows this to be his way. But he rarely leaves it behind after the drying. Almost never, really. And through their second progressive falling out, they have kept them on, their rings. Letting that be a thing.

She humphs at herself over this train of thought. *That is simply a ring left on a fucking basin.*

She steps into the shower.

Several minutes later Howard does not notice when she emerges from the bathroom clutching the too-flimsy, too-small bath towel to herself. He has opened the bedroom balcony door and has stepped out to try to do what he is usually adept at doing: managing his mind. Trying to distance himself from the emotional import of this trip, from the mutual pissiness he and Amanda sometimes are prone to, distance himself even from the twist his story took this evening, another thing altogether. All of it a welter in his head.

And now voices. A man and a woman a few balconies along the way to his right and one floor down, roiling upward into him like memory. But they are French voices. Angry at each other.

A couple struggling.

This is not helping.

He turns away.

Inside, Amanda has had time to slip out of her towel and into her pajamas—keeping her underlying nakedness to herself.

As she lies down, she too hears the voices.

She thinks: *When they perhaps are on the verge of parting forever, they'll have the same balcony view as ours to consider it.*

Howard steps back into the room.

Amanda pulls the covers over herself.

"Will it disturb you if I shower?" he asks.

"Not at all."

"All right then," he says.

He remembers to carry his pajamas with him into the bathroom. As he disrobes, he notices his wedding ring on the basin and makes a mental note to put it back on after the shower, a resolve that he will indeed remember ten minutes from now.

In the meantime, after he is naked and beneath the running water, he too is struck motionless by a commonplace thing. He reaches for the shower soap in the wire dish on the wall.

It is a bath-size bar of Ivory, still wet from Amanda's shower. Very familiar to his eye. Made present in every bathroom he has ever shared with her. But what holds him now in particular are the several long strands of her hair undulantly adhering to the bar. Discreetly darkened hair. She does that still, though not to the original late-night darkness of her Chaumont days.

He tries instinctively to alter the growing complexity of the moment.

He picks up the bar of wet soap.

He rubs a thumb across the hair to remove it.

It does not move.

He tries to press more deeply with his thumb.

It does not move.

He uses more fingers, uses his palm, tries all of that over again under the running water, and it barely rearranges Amanda's hair clinging to the soap.

All of this, he convinces himself, he has done as a practical matter.

But he abandons the effort and lathers and bathes to completion, and when he places the bar of Ivory soap in the dish for the last time, the hair remains.

Soon Howard and Amanda are lying beside each other in their separate beds with simultaneous jet lag. Awake for a further hour and reading each other's middle-of-the-night consciousness from their old-couple experience: Her restless feet beneath the covers. His spates of sniffing against balky sinuses.

Each has a moment when they think to ask, *Are you okay?* Each would do so partly from veiled irritation but also partly from quotidian spousal concern.

Though neither speaks.

And finally they sleep.

☙

On this debut night of tale-telling they eat simply—even microwaveably, with a nod of apology to the city beyond their balcony—but they have worked late, keeping French dinner hours, and so when they pull two of the cross-back side chairs from the table to face each other before their balcony doors, the sky to the west has completed its fade to black.

They sit.

Amanda opens her MacBook on her lap.

She finished writing not much more than an hour ago, and since then, she's been tweaking and polishing but also refraining. Refraining from consequential cuts and undercuts. Rightly refraining, she thinks now, in this moment of exposing her laptop screen and its story as if she's slipping out of her nightie. When done right, her writing process exposes her. She channels her words; she does not will them. And she has been pleased to find that this aspect of her process is fully alive even without her artistic license and with a dedication to full, literal truth, as much as possible given the quirks of memory and the vagaries of perception.

She lifts her eyes beyond her computer screen and into Howard's eyes. Which are watching her. Widened just a little. Steady. Howard showing his intelligence there. Showing his interest in a thing that he will be able to mull and deconstruct and reconstruct. To which he can give what his gang calls a *close read*.

She looks back down, stares again at the opening paragraph. She knows this first story needs to help define the form for the two of them. So she returns her eyes to Howard and says, "By my feelings now—*both* of ours—there are things here I would've overlooked in the writing or would've cut pre-dawn this morning. Tender things that fifty years later have more or less vanished or been transformed into something else. But that would be false. This tale lives in 1968. When it was true."

"I understand," he says.

"Okay then," she says.

She begins to read.

THE FIRST TALE
Amanda

Howard wielded our precious, borrowed key and opened the door. We stepped in, and while he locked the door behind us, I went on inside, across the living room to the French doors with their tiny Juliet balcony. The curtains were open but the windows were closed. Beyond and below was the sound that drew me. Dampened a bit but still distinct. Voices shouting in the Rue Guisarde, approaching, moving quickly past and then away, immediately having nothing to do with us.

The student and worker uprising of 1968 had begun to surge in Paris, intending drastically to change the government, change the economy. Our street was narrow and not much more than a hundred yards from one end to the other, cramped and unstrategic. But a four-minute stroll away was the Boulevard Saint-Germain, and the roar from there today was intensifying, shortly to have ten thousand student voices chiming in to riot, their uproar vivid even three hundred yards away and up three floors and through the window glass.

Howard and I were in this apartment as enlistees in an uprising of a different sort.

We were juniors at the Sorbonne. After briefly joining the student union protests, the alternative cause we decided to take up at the university was gender segregation, established with admission of the first female students in the nineteenth century and unrevoked, unmodified since.

Taking to the streets seemed an inappropriate mode of protest for this. So instead, Howard and I, one each of the two oppressed genders, had finally found a place in Paris to freely and fully fuck.

A righteous fight for a cause, sans tear gas and police batons. And with benefits.

We had known each other for four months, having

failed to meet in the fall term. Though I'd noticed Howard from afar, all right, an arresting figure of 1968-vintage young manhood, but with his own kind of strut, as if Jumpin' Jack Flash had been born in a library carrel instead of a cross-fire hurricane.

And he had seen something in me.

I closed the curtains on the French doors, and I turned to him. He was not strutting. Or even posing. He was simply standing still and looking at me intently from across the room.

Until now our relationship had found its expression only incompletely, in the dark, on a deserted stretch along the Quai des Grands Augustins, the two of us upright, with his trench coat opened and wrapped around us. We had a night-shadow relationship of hands and mouths on the bank of the Seine beneath the shuttered bookstalls.

But his older brother's friend from their hometown, a postgraduate student, had decamped to the South of France with wife and young child, anticipating how bad the student troubles would become in Paris. And he loaned us the key to this private space.

So with the curtains closed, I began to cross the room to Howard. Though he was adept at both strutting and cogitating demonstrably for my approval, he was instead maintaining a demeanor I had not yet seen in him. A great and serious stillness.

Given what we were about to do, I liked that. I was glad he'd saved it for now.

I stopped before him.

The stillness remained.

We looked at each other for a long moment.

I said, "You are non-bookishly serious. Strikingly so."

"I am," he said.

"This is new to me," I said.

I waited for him to respond. Only for a few seconds. If I'd had to wait longer, I might have begun to worry about what, in fact, was happening in him.

But in the nick of time he smiled. A small, slow, slightly lopsided, conspiratorial smile.

"It's new to me, as well," he said. "And yes, *serious*. I find myself abruptly persuaded that what we are about to begin will be serious."

He offered his hand.

I took it.

All of which, I realize, sounds analytical in him. In us. Passionless.

Perhaps it *was* a bit analytical. But it wasn't passionless.

Once in the iron bed in the next room, this man who was on top of, beneath, to the front, to the rear, beside me was neither the cogitator nor the strutter. He was active, but often, I need to add, overly meticulous. He lingered, but then sometimes was oddly rushed. He was oblivious to his surroundings. Including me, it occasionally seemed. But he had moments of looking me closely in the eyes. He was ardent. And he was at times overtly delighted in his work. Indeed, in this undertaking he displayed all the qualities that would someday be the distinctive and mostly admirable hallmarks of his scholarship.

And he was endearing.

I responded rather completely to all of that. Perhaps I did not hear bells or birds or a heavenly choir of cloned Willie Nelsons singing in his tender mode. But I assumed that was because the steeples and trees and choir lofts just a few blocks away were occupied, instead, by the sounds of struggle and clash between gendarmes and students. Quite clear to us in our iron bed. This was the theme music to the first episode of our full intimacy.

I chronicle all this with certainty. But the rhetorical mode of my account pains the novelist in me. I have described the first time that Howard and I made love in summarizing, generalizing terms, forsaking my primary métier: a rendering of the body's senses in the moment, in a fully realized scene. I have failed to fully inhabit myself and Howard and thus recreate our act as we experienced it. I am capable of plausibly *inventing* all that, with an appropriate novelistic immediacy. But I haven't done that either.

Because I find the *forgetting* is part of the story. The forgetting of our first fully realized act of lovemaking. I remember its affect accurately, I am sure, but I have lost the moment-to-moment thereness.

However, I have not forgotten the postcoital glow of that day and how it emboldened us, whispered to us of twenty-something immortality. Howard and I basked thus in the open French doors, pressed against Juliet's balustrade and each other, with just our outer layer of clothes restored. Though from the direction of the colonnaded warren of market halls down where our little street ended, from out beyond, from the Boulevard Saint-Germain, came the continuing distant clash and cry of street riot.

Our street itself was silent.

But we were both listening to what we knew was history being made within earshot.

Howard slipped his arm around me, cupping my hip in his palm. "Should we go back out there with them?"

I shook my head gently *no* at him: "We decided together it would be this instead. The politics of that bed in there have directly to do with us." I flipped my head a little back in the direction of the uproar: "That does not."

"I don't know," he said. "We can protest on two fronts."

"Fine. But not on this day."

"We can."

"You don't actionably mean it," I said.

"I do," he said, furrowing his brow.

"Your hand," I said.

He executed an I-don't-get-it cock of the head.

"On my hip. It's still clinging there."

"Ah," he said, removing it.

"Sweetly so," I said.

And to his credit, he confessed, "But it reveals me to be an unreliable narrator. Unconcerned with the second front."

"Put it back please."

He did.

And now a faint but unmistakable flypaper scent of tear gas wafted past us. We'd come to know that smell.

We both lifted our faces to it.

I said to Howard, "For us, though, the two protests are already linked. The sound of a mob or the smell of tear gas will forever evoke our Paris romance."

"One way or another," he said.

I looked at him, very briefly uncomprehending.

He read me. And he explained, "Forever evoke contentment at its having endured or regret at its having eventually ended."

Because I'd referred strictly to the former—at that moment on the balcony the only option for our romance

I could envision—I bristled inside. Bristled enough to say, "Or evoke cynicism at its having turned quickly to shit."

Even above the distant clamor I heard the abrupt suck and cease of Howard's breath at this.

I froze too. In regret. Howard and I had argued in these first few months together. Even a couple of heated arguments. But never with a comprehensively summarizing body blow such as this one.

Not that he hadn't prepared the way for it. I just never for a moment believed he meant to devalue our possible romantic hopes. His was the brain of a budding scholar compulsively close-reading. I thrashed in my head for the words to back us out of this rhetorical wrong turn.

I might even have begun to stammer, unawares, for he leaned a little toward me now. His hand had remained on my hip and this time he knew why. It gave me a small squeeze. "No more words," he said.

He turned me now and drew me alongside of him, and he led me from the balcony and across the living room and into the bedroom.

This time I will not even summarize the sex, the details of which, in our second session in the iron bed, have vanished down the same brain burrow as the details of the first session.

Ah, except for one brief episode.

And it made all the difference.

I was on my back. He was on his knees now, having risen directly above me, facing me, between my legs. He had no doubt already placed his strutting part within me. It is relevant that I can only assume the latter to be so.

But I can clearly see how I have lifted my hips and extended my legs against him, and I followed the line of them up his chest—how pallid my legs were—and they rested their inelegantly-named Achilles tendons on his collarbones. And the lift of all this climaxed with my toes, one set of which was behind each of his two ears, framing Howard's head like King Tut's crown. Especially so since I had painted their nails Max Factor Breezy Peach for the occasion and they went quite admirably with Howard's sweetly oversized ears.

In this position I awaited a drumming from him, albeit—by the example of our previous session—a scrupulously, indeed tenderly, moderated one.

I waited some more.

He also waited, looking me in the eyes from above, not moving any part of him.

And now his head shifted—lolled even—to the right, and he laid it against the side of my left foot. He closed his eyes, seemed to concentrate on this unexpected but clearly pleasant encounter of flesh on flesh.

I received the mood of this like an embrace.

We settled together into the moment.

Then his eyes opened.

His gaze fell upon me, briefly but comprehendingly.

He pulled away from my foot and took it in his hand and moved it gently forward a few inches, flexing my leg slightly at the knee.

He turned his face to my foot.

He leaned to it, and he put his mouth there, on its arch, touched me softly on the arch of my foot with his mouth. With his lips parting he touched me there, and with the tip of his tongue he caressed me, and now he dilated his lips into a full and lingering kiss.

And I keenly sensed this to be true even as it was

happening, a truth that would only be confirmed in the years to come: There was no fetish in this act. No kink. This was simply so: Along with all the other parts of me, he loved the very feet I walked on.

❧❧

On that note, Amanda sits back in her chair. Whatever that note actually was: In the reading of her tale aloud she has only now heard its climax, as if for the first time, the incident having been visited upon her very near the writing deadline. And yes. His kiss was an actual memory. An actual kiss. Her actual interpretation of the kiss at the time.

But now, her having written the kiss, having read it aloud, a question murmurs itself into her: *In sex when does tender become tepid?*

Which she answers: *Of course sex can be genuinely tender. Often should be.*

And then: *But it can be less.*

She cannot remember him ever doing it again.

And she finally accepts the ambiguity of that final act of his in her tale. Accepts it as being sweet, really, though also eccentric, odd somehow, and she thinks that the tone of her whole tale has been like the arch of the foot she insists he loved: smooth when stretched straight but wrinkled at the slightest flex.

Meanwhile, Howard leans back heavily, lifting his chair's front legs off the floor, pausing the chair and himself with the balls of his feet at a delicately sensed angle that seems to risk a fall over backward without, in fact, risking a fall over backward. Rather like the balancing act of his wife's tale, he thinks, tightroping between legitimate affection and long-enduring criticism.

"Well," he says.

"Don't forget …" she begins.

36

She pauses briefly. Calmly. Trying to find just the right words to finish her thought, for she knows that Howard, a professional subtexter, has already heard much that will niggle at him.

"Yes?" he prompts. "Forget?"

"Yes," she says. "Don't forget I was falling in love with you in that apartment."

"Ah," he says. "A nice thing not to forget."

"Yes."

"I will try."

"Try?"

"Not to. Seeing as the choir of Willie Nelsons did not sing."

"Oh that. It was the tumult on the Boulevard Saint-Germain."

"That should have been but background irrelevance," he says. "Readily forgotten." And Amanda is surprised at the tonal drag in his voice that suggests he's serious. Surely not.

He adds, "And you don't even remember the doing of the primary deed. Either time."

He is serious.

She says, "I wouldn't even want a choir of Willies for that. As solitary tang, his voice is fine. But a choir of them? Please."

"The expectation of a choir was *your* trope, my dear."

"Am I really giving you performance anxiety? Five decades after the fact?"

"Ha! *Fact* you say. The fact of a forgettable performance."

"Let me copy edit," she says. "Five decades after the *fuck*. After simply the event itself. My memory could well be the cause instead of your technique."

"There's related criticism throughout your tale, as well," he says. "I did not then understand that the bar had already been set."

And something clicks in her.

She almost says—almost—the words that are blooming in her. But she knows to simply think them: *These were the other heated arguments of our first months together. Not over performance anxiety. Over your jealousy. Your crazy, backward-looking, every-past-dick-is-still-a-rival jealousy. The couple of boys in my past I would be foolish enough to allude to later in our courtship.*

She thought he'd let all that go years ago. This is the worst possible time, place, and circumstance for him to regress.

Amanda is growing weary of this.

She very briefly gauges the space between the still back-ward-leaning Howard and the nearest immovable object behind him. With a mind to putting a toe under one of the lifted legs on his chair and giving it a flip.

But she isn't sure where his head would land. She just wants to dump him on his ass, not brain him.

So she says, "That tale as a whole was affectionate. More. It was loving, you idiot."

And he says, though gently, "I could hear the love, you bitch."

He drops his chair's front legs to the floor.

"Well, good," she says.

"Yeah, good," he says.

There was a time in this second marriage—perhaps as recently as a year or two ago—when they would now smile at each other, perhaps even chuckle together, after an argument. Though the conditions that would prompt such a mutual response are mostly the same at the moment, and though Amanda and Howard are even more or less aware of those conditions, they do not smile and they do not chuckle. They do feel a small bloom of relief, however, that there will likely be no more rancor tonight.

Amanda does pat Howard's knee in passing, as she rises from her chair, and he reaches after her hand, but too late, gently groping only empty air.

He is content with her touch. And she is content with the intention of his touch.

March 20, 2020

Howard awakes, Amanda snoring as she has always done—a slow, thoughtful inhalation and a slow, slightly burbling exhalation. He has slept only a few hours but feels fully revived and compelled to work on his tale. He has heard his literary wife's first story and he is reminded that a literary scholar's close read, though a step in the right direction, is not the same as what a literary writer might well call *close writing*. Howard knows he need not, should not, cannot engage his own core process as reader, as scholar, as academic writer. He needs to understand what he is about to do—with regard to *process*—as a fundamentally different thing.

To begin with, it is best for him to creep from their bedroom. To covertly slip into that thoughtless—and he means no disparagement in that word but simply, literally, *without conscious, abstract thought*—slip into that same thoughtless place where his wife says her own core process operates.

And their plan is actually even more comfortable for him, that it's literary in its rendering but in content he's looking for the unaltered truth.

Creep he does.

He sits before his computer at the dining table.

He started his story where his wife had started hers, though he soon went elsewhere. All this was so prior to hearing hers last night.

He reads the first sentence, a remnant of his slow early-going.

In the late spring of that year we lived in separate dormitories at the Sorbonne, but while thousands of Maoists and Marxists, anarchists and Che Guevarists, revisionist socialists and situationist surrealists, three flavors of Trotskyists, and even a small garnish dish of Stalinists congregated in the Boulevard Saint-Germain to change the world, she and I lay together nearby, in a bed in an apartment on the Rue Guisarde.

And Howard criticizes himself audibly. Though softly, in deference to his first and second wife's oblivious sleep. "Starts out blatantly derivative," he says, "and quickly turns reflexively researchy."

But then he disputes himself aloud. "No. Read it again, more closely."

He does.

And he thinks, *The opening words are ironic literary allusion, not the appropriated voice of Hemingway. The rendering of the groups in the street are not political sums but a welter of students striving for personal meaning. Both things are thus perceived by and spoken through the felt personality of the narrator. Who happens to be me. Truly so.* Howard feels this to be legitimate, as both reader and would-be literary writer. But he recognizes at once that these are privileges he must take care not to abuse.

He feels he has not, in the 628 words he's written so far. After that first sentence his narrative lingers in the moment. And when it veers away at word 233, it is in a righteously aesthetic direction, he thinks. The truth can be aesthetic, too. But he has been kept awake tonight by the impulse to veer again in what comes next. He must be careful.

And in that spirit he makes a mental note to stop doing word counts.

He has hours to go before he reads.

He puts his hands to the keyboard.

And the light comes, and the day, and through it all, he hardscrabbles out a few hundred more words. 515, actually, though to his credit he does not count them.

☙

Now it is evening.

The sky has again gone dark.

The ritual has been established: They move the cross-back chairs to the French doors.

Amanda sits before him, her hands folded in her lap.

Howard opens his MacBook.

He reads aloud that first sentence he vetted in the middle of the night. It sounds good. But after he places the two of them "in a bed in an apartment on Rue Guisarde," he pauses and glances over his screen at Amanda.

She immediately gives him a close read: "Don't think about an audience. Just inhabit your voice."

He tries to read *her*: *She hears a manifest voice in what I'm reading and I just need to trust it. Good.*

But he immediately reinterprets her comment. A *closer* read. And he cannot disentangle a suddenly glaring ambiguity in his head. She *might*, in fact, mean that she hears the voice of a head-bound academic self-consciously trying—and failing—to imitate a literary writer. She's offering advice for the next story. This one's lost from the start.

Or not.

For now he prefers to keep all that ambiguous.

So he begins to read on.

Amanda interrupts him. "Start over," she says. "Stories are whole objects."

And so he does.

ʕ؃

THE SECOND TALE
Howard

In the late spring of that year we lived in separate dormitories at the Sorbonne, but while thousands of Maoists and Marxists, anarchists and Che Guevarists, revisionist socialists and situationist surrealists, three flavors of Trotskyists, and even a small garnish dish of Stalinists congregated in the Boulevard Saint-Germain to change the world, she and I lay together nearby in an apartment on the Rue Guisarde.

We had just made love for the first time, fully and without clothes, in a bed. And now, after she offered an unnecessary but affecting apology for feeling compelled to do so, she has proceeded to fall asleep.

I lay beside her on my back. It was late afternoon. The room was dim. I could smell her. I could smell *us*. But the base note of her scent was the one she had given to herself. Patchouli. Straight, as an essential oil, bought in a Rive Gauche head shop and worn through all our touching. It was now restoring her post-coital body to sweet-turned earth and musk.

I tried to nap with her. I tried for long enough that my mind settled into my satedness and into my thwarted snooziness, but I could not actually sleep. The scent of her lingered in me as well, and all of this mingled and combined and surprised me as would a dream. I was carried somewhere I did not expect.

To Mama.

She sat at her dressing table.

She was facing the mirror.

She wore her slate blue kimono with the golden dragon climbing her back, its long crimson tongue curling up nearly to her shoulder.

Then the dragon slid quickly out of sight as my mother turned to me and beckoned me with the smallest but largest of smiles.

I climbed into her lap.

That moment might be my earliest memory of her, and though what I was experiencing in it was surely complete, what I can identify of it now in detail was certainly from later.

It was the scent of my mother.

She drew me close. "Howard little man," she said and she clutched me to her.

What I smelled was a perfume she would someday wear to her grave. Tabac Blond. A top note smell of tobacco. Cigarettes. Not lit, but as when they are huddled together in the pack. Or more precisely, as when they are all gone, after they've been lit and smoked and have vanished. The smell left in the empty pack. And another top note, just as strong, was a smell of leather. Tanned leather. Eventually I would think I recognized it in my first schoolbag. I carried her smell on my back for years, with my school books. And there were other Tabac Blond notes from her skin, from her embrace, but I identified them only quite a bit later in life, only after I encountered the smells elsewhere and they reminded me of her: vanilla and oak moss, carnation, and, yes, patchouli.

She smoked, my mother. This too is an early memory. I was no older than five. 1953. Maybe younger. The smell of her Marlboros was part of the mix of scents joining with her Tabac Blond. And Marlboros in those days were indeed blond tobacco, flue-cured to be mild for the women expected to smoke them. When Tabac Blond was created in 1924, it was to allure men but also to mask the smell of smoked tobacco on a trailblazing modern woman. Though even in the Fifties, Mama was still sometimes looked at critically for smoking. I suspect that she always wished she'd been born a generation earlier so she could have lit up even more defiantly, that she could have blazed a trail.

Tabac Blond was Marlene Dietrich's favorite perfume. She smoked famously.

My father was an insurance executive.

My mother, on the rare occasion that she tucked me into bed, would sing me to sleep. By its very rarity, wonderfully so. Always "Falling in Love Again," pitching her voice low, evoking Dietrich, who made it her theme song.

I clung to my mother. I breathed her in.

As a five-year-old I was not entirely faithful to her, however.

I was smitten with Princess Summerfall Winterspring on the primordial early Fifties television show *Howdy Doody*. No puppet strings for the princess. An actual human actress, though hardly a Native American, but with darkly arresting eyebrows and pullable, twistable, face-caressable braids.

Maybe those braids explain why the princess was my first crush. Mama sometimes did up her hair in braids. Though I realized later it was when the darkness came most upon her. I learned to stop at her bedroom door if she had her braids, when normally I would rush to her lap as she sat at her dressing table. The braids told me to hang back.

She would turn her face to me and her makeup would already be gone and the braiding, it seemed to me, had pulled her eyes and her mouth taut, which was the actual reason for the rictus of seeming sadness on her face. But no. The sadness was her own.

Whenever I've thought of the braided moments from those early years, one such has come to represent them all. Mama's cigarette is in her mouth. She does not remove it at the sight of me in the doorway. She does not touch it. The smoke curls up before her face as sinuous as a dragon's tongue. She says, "Not tonight, little man. Mama's weary." And I go.

Princess Summerfall Winterspring's braids were part of a goofy smile or a transparently put on, soon-banished frown or a giddy chirpiness. I sat before our Capehart Console Television and ardently felt the allure of this female before me—in the pre-carnal way a five-year-old boy sometimes can—made all the more intense by her chirpy braids offsetting Mama's despairing ones.

How wrong was Princess Summerfall Winterspring in several ways, all typical of 1953 white America: That thought made me blink back to the apartment in Paris and turn my face to Amanda sleeping beside me.

Her back was to me.

I drew nearer. Gently, so as not to disturb her.

Her hair was cut short. Along the back of her neck the line of the cut had grown ragged. I lifted a hand, brought a forefinger tip near, wanting to run it there. The public women of that time—like Farrow, Hepburn, Twiggy—when they cut their hair like this it was declared to be like a *pixie*.

I loved Amanda's hair.

She was no pixie.

The actress who played Princess Summerfall Winterspring died in a car accident in Wyoming in 1957 at the age of twenty-four.

My mother will die at her dressing table in the summer of 1965.

She will be wearing her slate blue kimono.

She and Amanda will never have met.

Howard closes his laptop and finds it hard to lift his eyes from the bitten apple icon on the lid. For all the foot-shuffling about what it is they are doing, now that Howard has read his story to his professional literary wife, he wishes simply to rise and leave the room. He is unaccustomed—to say the least   to impulses in himself of cringing deference. And there is some of that, even if hopeful, over the voice and flow of the words. But his hesitation runs deeper, now that he has heard what he wrote. Not that he wants to go there. He prefers to cringe over craft.

Amanda, too, sets aside the questions of a different sort. They are still ill-shaped, and her line-to-line response to him has surprised her.

Reading his demeanor, in a gently smiling voice she says, "Every writer I know, including me, feels this way. Often."

He still does not lift his eyes from the MacBook. As if of the lid, he asks, "Who the hell took the bite out of that apple? And why?"

Amanda carries on, retaining the tone of a smile: "A good start to overcome the feeling would be to look at me."

"Maybe it's a b-y-t-e bite?"

She sighs. She'll play his game for a moment or two: "I think I read somewhere the unbitten version of the apple looked like a cherry."

The longer Howard keeps his head down, the more deference feels to him like shame.

He looks her in the eyes.

But he keeps up the ruse: "Right. Who'd buy a Cherry Computer?"

Amanda says, "I've been waiting to see your eyes to tell you this. So listen."

She does not mean to pause. But for the briefest of moments she takes a breath and for that same fleeting moment his breath crimps sharply.

And she says, "I liked what you wrote. I liked it a lot. I was impressed."

She means it. He seems to know how to talk naturally to the page. Some of the time.

"No shit?" he asks.

"No shit," she says.

They let that sit for a moment.

He has begun to smile. Ever so slightly. If it were a larger smile she would let more time pass before she says what is next. But the very slightness of the smile—the of-course-that's-so of it; the that's-the-reaction-I-actually-expected of it—leads her to add now, instead of later: "I have to tell you how obvious and deep one writer's literary influence on you is."

"Hemingway?"

"No," she says. "Allusions to him, yes. Not actual rhythm-and-diction level influence."

"Who then?"

"Me."

She is braced.

But he simply goes unblinkingly still.

He's working out a rhetorical strategy, she figures.

He rolls his shoulders ever so slightly and says, "I can well imagine that's your highest compliment."

She thinks: *He's over his funk. Giving me an either-way-she-loses choice of replies. Yes it is my highest compliment. Or: No it is not my highest compliment. Yes I have overweening delusions of literary grandeur. Or: No I've failed at the foolishly highest aspiration of my youth.*

But then she thinks to say, "You need not *well imagine*. After all these years you know exactly what that means."

They both recognize how twenty-two-plus-nine years of feeling and talking and competing and striving and loving and losing it and finding it again and ending up baffled as hell over it can hijack conversations between them. They realize it has just happened.

A cumulative thirty-one years together have also taught them to just shut down the snark for a while.

"A glass of wine?" Howard says.

"Yes," Amanda says.

Howard rises. "I'll pour."

"I'll open the windows." Amanda rises.

"Our French doors," he says. "Ironic, yes? Our first set of them opened onto wildly noisy chaos."

He pauses very briefly to encourage her to collaborate on the point.

Which she does, though with a brief hesitation. "And our … present set opens to a plague of silence."

It is clear to them both that she has almost said the obvious, neatly bookending thing: And our *final* set …

But she caught herself.

They both heard the ending of another marriage in the unspoken locution. Unintended as a reference. Not exactly feared as a possibility, but not necessarily desired. So they have evaded it. And they will ignore it.

For now.

Instead, they will continue to tell tales till the plague passes by.

But next, a glass of wine.

Which they have several of until they are lying in parallel, in their two beds, in the dark, slow to sleep, listening to each other breathe.

He clears his throat. A quickie. By the sound of it, unnecessary.

Amanda says, softly, "Are you awake?"

"Yes."

"Awake enough to chat?"

They have not spoken again of Howard's tale.

But as they have engaged the nightly wooing of their unconscious, the other stuff of the story has started to stir in them both.

Which is where she is going, and he suspects as much. "Yes," he says. "If you want."

"I do."

"No obligation," he says.

"I know that."

She lets a few beats of silence pass before she says, "You've hardly ever talked about your mother."

"No, I haven't."

"Was I always supposed to ask about her?"

"You were always supposed to ask about anything you wanted."

Amanda hears herself. "It sounds like I'm picking a fight," she says.

"Yes."

"I'm sorry. I really don't mean to."

A rustle of his pillow. He's turned his face to her, she thinks.

She looks toward him. The ambient light from curtain edge and clock face show very little. The shape of their heads. Just a darkness for the eyes they seek.

But for both of them that's okay. They continue to look.

"Thanks for clarifying," he says. "About the fight."

"The non-fight," she says.

"The non-fight."

Part of Amanda wants to elaborate on her provocative question, now that she has apologized for its tone. She wants to say: *I always got the impression I shouldn't ask.* But it's too risky. She wants no more fights tonight. Even of the non-fight variety.

She asks instead, "Do you think about her?"

"Not often."

"*Think* isn't the word I mean," she says.

In the silence that follows, in the masking darkness, she abruptly worries that even this might start a new wrangle. He typically doesn't distinguish thinking from feeling.

Though he made a start at that with his story.

Which he continues. "Yes," he says. "I catch her scent. More often than think about her."

She likes this. But for the very reason she likes it, she doesn't quite know how to follow up on it. So she gets as close as she can. "You knew her perfume so well. How did you learn?"

She hopes he'll go even further, hopes he'll say *By smelling her.* And then—perhaps empowered by the dark and their shared drowsiness—he'll tell a full story about her, with the perfume and the tobacco as simply background scents rather than her fading into the background while Tabac Blond and Marlboros are featured in miniature monographs.

But he says, "I learned her perfume through my first extended act of scholarship. I recognized it as a child, her scent and all, but when I came into my teens I began to study what I breathed in. I researched it. Till I truly understood."

Howard falls silent. QED.

Amanda has nothing more to say. She knows when he's found shelter in his head. *The scholar's blessed QED: Quod Erat Demonstrandum. Confidently understood and clearly demonstrated.*

Besides. Just this much talk has made them both as sleepy as they should have been all along.

But as Amanda begins to submit to her will to sleep, Howard's mama presents herself, sitting at her dressing table in braids, her face shrouded in cigarette smoke. And Amanda now recalls—and accepts as certain—her fleeting suspicion of the subtextual truth in Howard's tale: *His mother took her own life.* Which leads back to Amanda's thoughts of the lit-crit paradigm at work: Smell first and then just analyze the hell out of it. Unto QED. Does Howard even *know* what his mother did? It happened when he was off at Yale in their summer session, as a gifted high schooler, a few weeks before he turned seventeen. His father—the shadowy insurance man—no doubt discovered her. Perhaps kept the truth from him.

Meanwhile Howard expects to complete his move toward sleep in his accustomed way, repeating rhythmically in his head a monthly refreshed literary phrase. Presently, from Steinbeck: "the high grey-flannel fog of winter." But instead, Howard's mother appears before him wrapped in a gray-silk fog of cigarette smoke. She sits at her dressing table. He stands at the door. She has turned to him in her chair and he knows the sadness is upon her and he expects her to send him away. But he waits at least for a few words. *Not tonight, little man.* But she says nothing. She simply turns her back to him, and he takes this as permission. He steps into her bedroom and begins to cross the floor. And as he moves he realizes he is not her little man. He is tall. He is fully a man. He is moving toward his mother and she leans forward at her dressing table and lays her head there.

He thinks: *She is weary.*

He arrives beside her.

He touches her on the shoulder.

She does not move.

She is dead. His mother is dead.

He has no conscious suspicion.

And Howard is asleep.

But Amanda will carry this night into her dreams. She spent this past day working on what she intended to be her next tale. About her first inspiration to write. But after only a few hours of sleep, her father beckons her from across the room, beckons her to step up onto his shoes and dance with him.

March 21, 2020

   In the morning light Amanda brings her coffee back to the table. Ever since her father appeared to her she has been writing an alternate tale. She expects this to be the last cup. Howard's morning appearance will restore the bedroom as her writing space. And, on this day, a few-hour nap space.

   She sits. She looks at the most recent words on her laptop screen. She takes her first sip. Puts down the mug. Bends to the keyboard.

   Howard: "How long …?"

   His voice jolts her upright, her hands flipping up as if before a thief with a pistol.

"Sorry," he says.

Amanda turns to him, composes herself.

"I thought of clearing my throat," he says.

"Same result, I'm sure."

"Sorry anyway."

"All night," she says. "In answer to what I assume you were asking."

"No wonder you jumped."

"It wasn't the coffee."

"Is there any left?"

There is. She lets her irritation go.

And the two of them sit at the table.

They sip together in silence and try, while nonchalantly avoiding an engagement of eyes, to comprehend each other.

Howard is struck by her state—the midst of creation—which he does not recall having interrupted this clearly before.

Amanda—reminded now that her father has come upon her by way of Howard's mother—feels words growing in her that she wishes to speak to him but finds she can only think: *You and your mother inspired this change in the tale I'm now writing about my father. She inspired you to find the possibility of a real writer in you. Do you know your mother committed suicide? At least does your nascent artistic unconscious know? It was missing in your first tale, though we learned a great deal about her perfume. Which was emotional in its own way, I recognize, but expressive of an averting of your eyes. Your eyes right now. Not just your eyes back then. A footnote for you, my scholarly husband: From Akira Kurosawa, who once said, "To be an artist means never to avert your eyes."*

But she keeps that to herself. She cannot play his game.

Finally she does say, "I should go now. You need the table."

"You must be tired."

"I am. And you need to write."

"I do," he says.

Amanda rises.

Howard has an impulse to reach to her hand—simply to touch it as she is about to go—but the impulse surprises him and he pauses to consider the gesture, analyze it, and she is gone.

☙

That evening, she and Howard sit down across from each other in their accustomed places. Amanda is ready to read, her midmorning nap having been sufficient to sustain—and perhaps even, in its dream-laden brevity, facilitate—the creative zone that produced the rest of her story.

Howard settles back in his chair and, with what feels to him to be a sympathetic smile, crosses his arms on his chest. As she begins to read.

৵৹৻

THE THIRD TALE
Amanda

We are legion, I strongly suspect. The women who were girls who danced upon their fathers' shoes. Who believed they were dancing with him when, in fact, they were no more dancing than they were running when they were snatched up by their mothers and carried quickly from the house where things had just gone very wrong.

Only to come back, for the most part. In those days, in the era when I was a child, even the actual going away was pretty rare. The staying away was rarer.

We came back.

I danced again on his shoes.

The offense was against her. Not me. Though it might as well have been, for I loved her.

But I loved him too.

He and I danced.

My feet were bare. He said I was learning. He moved in dance steps, with me standing there, reaching up to hold his hands.

Yes. I was learning. But not to dance.

To feel.

I knew my father through the bottoms of my feet. My toes lay on the vamp of his Oxfords, cool and slick. And I felt the imprint of the wingtips of his shoes, the wings sweeping beneath me and joining like the tips of arrows at the balls of my feet.

He danced with me upon him. And beneath each of my feet were dozens of holes, seen as part of the wingtip and upper pattern but felt as pixelated negative space now that they were so close to me. My father danced with feet punctured into emptiness.

And yet. He held my hands. He held my gaze. Nat King Cole sang "When I Fall in Love" on our Silvertone. I lifted toward my father. And we danced. To my ardent yearning. To my unmistakable shame. As if I were betraying my mother.

We lost him eventually, my mother and I. Later. When my bare feet would no longer fit on the vamp and upper of his shoes. I was too tall simply to hold his hands and gaze at him far above. For a time those felt like the reasons. I assumed he left us because I could no longer be his precious little girl. And I felt a shame of a different sort. A self-absorbed one.

But the reality was that Papa finally fucked one too many other women. The whole thing was between three people. I just wasn't one of them.

Except of course I was.

After he was gone, when Mama was at her work, I would sometimes put Nat King Cole on the record player. And I would dance. For a time it was as if with my father.

But not for long. I figured him out, fully, once and for all. I felt ashamed once more. And then I let him go.

As if such things ever really end, even if the father and daughter involved never see each other again. As if the way it did continue would be easily recognizable for what it was.

Kathleen Higgins and I, barely fifteen, danced together at the Wausau High School freshman hop. There were a dozen female dancing couples, with many of the boys of Wausau inadequate on the dance floor for the fast numbers, the DNA of their Upper Wisconsin lumberjack ancestors sabotaging their moves and making the jitterbug impossible for them.

Kathleen was taller than me. She would dance the boy's role. She wouldn't let me apologize. *I like to spin you*, she would say. *I like you to spin me*, I would say. And we danced. We'd been practicing together in her bedroom since junior high. Her parents had money and she was an only child. Her room was large. Or we practiced in my living room, in front of *American Bandstand* on the television. The practicing was with an air and a focus that was a mid-century girl's sublimated professionalism. But in our socks, on the gymnasium floor, actually doing our Underarm Turns and our Inside Turns and eventually learning to do the Cuddle Step, we were no longer channeling professionalism. Our sublimation shifted its venue.

We'd just learned the Cuddle for the freshman Thanksgiving dance.

"What will they think?" I asked Kathleen, low, leaning near as we sat together on the bleachers with the rest of our class cliqued about us. She knew I was talking about our doing the Cuddle.

"What do we care?" she said.

"We don't," I said.

"We don't."

And soon the DJ put on "Chantilly Lace," a good jitterbug tune, and Kathleen and I were on the floor together and we were stepping to each other and away, to and away, and we did an Underarm Turn and we stepped some more and we were looking each other in the eyes and saying with them *Why wait?* and we took both our hands and we stepped left and we stepped right and we rock stepped back, staying in place, and Kathleen lifted my right hand with her left and she spun me and my back was to her and we kept holding our hands and she pulled me into her, our arms entwined, and then I was pressed against her at her side, our adjoining shoulders and arms overlapping, my upper arm snug against her left breast, and we did not let go, we rock stepped and rock stepped again and again, and our bodies were side by side and cuddled close.

Did we draw looks? I don't know. Probably. But that wasn't why we did it. To have checked to see, to have even wondered for more than a moment about that, would have been to spoil it. We did the Cuddle Step twice more to the Big Bopper's vocals in our first dance. We did it for us. And we did it at least once in every jitterbug they played.

That evening, the Bopper was the focus of a laugh that Kathleen and I shared as we discovered irony, though we didn't discover the label. We were in our accustomed private space, her bedroom. Her parents weren't home after the dance and my mother knew not to worry—or had stopped worrying—about my comings and goings when Kathleen was involved. The laugh was for how the Big Bopper's vocals sounded like somebody's father, though he was twenty-seven when he recorded our cuddle song. Laughed at his having a leering, heavy voice, an old voice. A forty-year-old's voice. We laughed at that even as we thanked him for the background music to the Cuddle Step done by a couple of early-teen girls, and then we both cut the laughter off sharply, simultaneously.

How in tune was our thinking that night. We stopped laughing because it struck us that he was dead, J. P. Richardson, The Big Bopper from Port Arthur, Texas. Dead a few years already. Dead along with Buddy Holly and Ritchie Valens in a plane crash when we were still in junior high.

I knew this is what had struck us both. I knew it even before Kathleen said, "How sad, you know?"

"He died," I said.

"Yes."

"And the others."

"Have you ever had someone die?"

"Mama says Papa is dead to us," I said. "But that's not the same."

"Why haven't we talked about this?"

"I didn't have anyone."

"I had a cousin," Kathleen said. "My age."

"I'm sorry."

"I don't want to miss anything," she said. "In my life."

I nodded. It wasn't what I'd expected. But she was right. I liked my friend Kathleen more, for saying this. "Me either," I said.

"We can still improve our Cuddle Step," she said.

This surprised me too. That instant leap from early death to the dance. I probably could not have found words for what I thought was her reason, but I said yes at once because somehow I understood. The dancing was life. It was the answer to the death of twenty-somethings who sang the songs we danced to.

"Want to practice it some more?" she said.

"Now?"

"Sure."

I heard her speaking to our professionalism. To escape a feeling for death by a feeling for this. I adored my friend Kathleen. "Yes," I said.

She moved straight to the center of the floor. She usually went first to the record player.

"No music?" I asked.

"We can concentrate on the move," she said.

So we stood before each other.

We took each other's hands and we began to dance, going through the motions slowly. With Kathleen counting the beat in a low voice, we stepped and then stepped and then rock stepped and Kathleen lifted my right arm and she spun me gently and she was behind me and pulling me toward her and our hands and our arms were folded all together around me and I began to angle toward her left side to cuddle along that side of her to proceed with the dance.

But Kathleen guided me back toward her. Toward the

center of her. And she pulled me to her. And I pressed my body fully against hers. Her breasts to my shoulder blades. Her hips fitting just above my bottom. Her hands still holding mine but staying upon me, crossing upon my chest.

The forward moving dance steps ceased.

We continued to rock for a time, minutely, side to side. Full-body cuddling. Letting that step truly earn its name.

Then I asked her with my body to let me turn. She released my hands and I stayed very very near but I turned to face her, and my mind had drifted, as if I were alone in bed and the room was dark and I wished to sleep but I'd been unable to and now at last I could and the drift carried me and I looked into Kathleen's hazel eyes and they seemed bizarrely complicated to me, green and brown and blue, and her arms came around me and I put my arms around her, and Kathleen bent to me and I sensed what she wanted and I rose that brief distance that made her the man in our dancing.

And our lips touched.

And we kissed.

I knew at once my kiss was about Kathleen. Solely about her.

Body deep, this kiss, but then I knew it was about friendship. Just that. And about this one very specific moment.

But a fine moment.

Our lips parted and I kissed her once more.

And that was all.

It would go hard for the two of us. For the following hour. For the following weeks. That it should be two kisses and no more.

Sadly, I never found the right words while Kathleen Higgins still lived in Wausau. We stopped being together. We stopped looking at each other as we passed in the hall.

She and her family were gone the following year.

Her father's job, I heard.

I let her go.

It would be a few years—with me sadly replaying all that she and I were and weren't to each other—for me to finally figure out what to say to her. As a clear explanation, which she deserved. And I said it to her in my head many times over the coming years. Feeling comfortable now at last to begin *My darling Kathleen.* And then: *The kiss was like our dancing together. We loved each other as two girls dancing together in their socks can love each other. Which is a very strong love. But I was waiting for the dumbbell boys to catch up. Waiting for some dumbbell to turn into a fully functioning man. How sad is that? But that's who I am. A given. If I had been different in that way, then it would have been you and me instead. How sad.*

Amanda stares at her laptop screen.

Yes, there's a flicker left in her of something tender and lost and impossible. But then she feels Howard's eyes upon her and she keeps her own eyes on the screen. *How sad,* she thinks. *How sad, the things that made that moment with my friend impossibly complicated. The complications were mine. My genes and my hormones for starters, straight from Mama's womb, and then the big life-shapers—my home and my school and my church and my town, not to mention my fucked-up mid-twentieth-century America. How sad, the wicked-deep biases and limitations that all those things laid into me.*

And this is too much for Amanda now, staring at a computer screen after way too little sleep over the past thirty-six hours. She willfully sets the complications aside and thinks, *How sad indeed. Dumbbell boys. Dumbbell men. They too are legion. Utterly forever, unable to dance. Unable to take leave of their own brains and bodies and empathize into ours and let us into theirs likewise. Thus to dance. To really dance. Together.*

And she waits to lift her eyes. And she thinks, *I have oversimplified it, though as far as the limits go, not inaccurately.*

So she looks into the eyes of her very own dumbbell.

He's not showing much.

And she tells herself what she has always tried to tell herself: *He is of a special sort. Not strictly dumb. He simply cannot think and dance at the same time. No one can, for that matter. But whenever he can choose, it is always to think.*

He says, "I don't remember you mentioning your teenage crush."

He hesitates.

She has heard the twang of retroactive jealousy in his voice.

She feels herself ready to make a big deal of this. But she settles for a nuanced dig, blithely accepting his characterization: "My teenage crush? Haven't I mentioned her? Surely in thirty-one years together."

"I have a good memory," he says.

"Ah, that you do."

"You never spoke of her to me. Did you tell Daniella?"

Their daughter Dani.

Married now to Joanne.

"No," Amanda says. *Dani understood I deeply approved of her. Why go out of my way to tell her I broke someone's heart?*

Explaining this now only to herself.

She knows what Howard will ask next. He'll slide from their daughter back to his jealousy. He begins: "For you, was that …"

"Yes," Amanda says. "That was the only time."

She knows his next question, as well.

He begins: "With …"

"… any girl," she says. "The only time. The only kiss."

Howard's Adam's apple bounces at swallowing back any further words—as she is doing—and, perhaps as well, Amanda hopes, he is swallowing down a bit of his jealousy like a bit of food stuck at the back of his throat.

She does, however, feel a mitigating ripple about Howard: His present jealousy is fully gender-equal, gender-acceptant. He has always been sincerely good about Dani's sexual identity.

So she says no more. It is up to Howard to advance the conversation.

But he simply murmurs some end-of-day boilerplate, and they go off to prepare for sleep.

Later, in the bed, the lights barely out, Amanda having just finished arranging her covers, Howard finally says, "The story was good."

She does not reply.

"Really," he says.

"Thank you," she says.

There is a beat of silence.

Amanda feels her consciousness fading away with the flicker of a question—*What took him so long to compliment me?*—and an answering flicker—*His own agenda, of course.*

A moment later he says, "Good night." And then, "I meant it. I was moved."

No response.

He realizes she has not heard this further compliment.

She is asleep now.

He regrets that. "Fuck me," he whispers, at not having said this earlier.

And he thinks, *I can even imagine a scholarly paper on how the Kathleen part of her story interrogates the Papa part.*

March 22, 2020

Just after midnight Howard awakes.

To his surprise he fell asleep quickly, though he'd gone to bed early simply to accompany her, that being the only collegial gesture he found himself capable of last evening. He was almost entirely silent after her story. Unable to speak. She surely did not know what to make of that. *He* has not yet figured out what to make of it. Now she is deep in sleep and he is awake in the dark and he can only talk with himself. Which he does, in his head.

She surprised me. Yes. I admit it. Shook me, even. Yes I admit briefly feeling a bit more than a niggle of jealousy about her. Over a fifteen-year-old girl. Amanda was willingly complicit in the kiss. And she repeated it. But I'm glad I didn't speak of this tonight. Not a word. She would have heard a classically over-the-top kind of male jealousy. Possessive. Even retroactively possessive. As: You're mine and you were always mine. Even before we met. Or even: What you gave to her is something I wanted from you for myself. What I wanted of your passion: The clean, the first, the untainted, the imprint made in your blood, in your body, so that whoever else you may ever kiss, the touch of my lips would always be there as well. My body. Indelible. That was something like me once, I admit. Something. Wanting that. Early on I showed that to Amanda. Openly fretting about her earlier boyfriends, what they'd done together, how immutably, irreplaceably memorable their closeness might have been. But in my distorted 1960s male desires, as inappropriate, as unconscionable as all of that is in the 2020s, it's not what I'm feeling now. Not even retroactively. Not even vicariously in this process of calling myself out.

Thinker that he is, he does briefly brainstorm the thought that these latter-day enlightened feelings might at least partially depend on the septuagenarian waning of his testosterone.

But he lets that go.

From a harder-won, more deeply engaged part of him, he addresses Amanda directly in his mind.

Now I'm stunned by what you may have lost. They were your kisses to give. And your Kathleen received them happily. Were you sure there could only be two of them? Were you right, even if you felt you were sure? Or were you as wildly wrong about who you were, who you should be, as I would have been about myself in 1962 if I'd known about that kiss? Or even if I'd known when I was with you in a borrowed apartment in Paris when we were twenty? When we first made love, I did not ask about earlier kisses because I dared not know. And did you avoid thinking about your Kathleen for the same reason? And our own daughter. Our own Daniella. Our Dani. Has she always been fully your daughter and you her mother in a way intrinsic to you as well? Did you abandon that same part of yourself? Have you carried a lost love ever since? Do you love Kathleen still?

This thought sits in Howard for a moment. And then: *This much is true. From your mothering, in its actionable fullness, our daughter has found her happiness with a woman. Which we know is the right and true and, indeed, the only way for her. Thank you for that. And maybe it wasn't the way for you yourself. Maybe you were absolutely right in turning away from Kathleen.*

Howard sits up.

He thinks to jump up.

But he holds back.

He begins to move, quietly so as not to disturb Amanda's sleep.

Her story—the story in full—has changed his own plans for tonight. Not changed. Inspired. In ways his usual mind does not understand.

Which is no doubt for the best.

He rises from his bed.

He will start a new story.

⚬

Amanda sleeps late, and when she wakes she is alone in the bedroom. She carries into consciousness sleep-mulled themes from last night: Kathleen, let go. Dani, embraced.

Life has gone its way, she thinks.

She sits up in the bed, puts her feet on the floor.

She tries to dispel last night's feelings about him. At least about the lingeringly adolescent Howard.

She rises into the gap, turns, looks around the tiny bedroom she shares with her husband. In effect, where they now live. The doors to the balcony comprise the wall to her left, to her right are the closet and the entrance door, and facing her beyond the foot of the bed, in a row, in the precious little remaining space, sit their two empty suitcases beside a chest of drawers and a wooden valet.

The latter is draped with Howard's shirt from yesterday. In its

67

tray are his crumpled socks and crumpled underwear.

Left to his own devices, Howard will eventually deal with those things.

But wherever the two of them have elsewhere lived, she has rarely waited for his own devices in such matters. So she puts his laundry in a cloth bag she's brought with her and hangs up his shirt.

Life has gone its way, she thinks once more.

When she emerges from the bedroom she quickly recognizes Howard's deadline-driven intensity. He is writing at the table. She slips past him without a word, in deference to his preoccupation. But she is also still conscious of the minimal conversation of the previous evening.

As she begins to make her coffee in the kitchen, Howard says, "Sorry. Can't talk for now. Like you, I started over in the middle of the night."

"Good for you," she says.

Minutes later, as she carries her coffee toward the bedroom to work on her own story, he stops her with a light hand on her free forearm. With his hand lingering there, even squeezing her gently, he begins to speak with scholarly admiration about the Kathleen part of her story interrogating the Papa part. Speaks with warmth.

Howard having emotions about thoughts, she thinks. *The integrated Howard.*

She would have appreciated a bit of that last night, but she tunes out his content now as her eyes follow his hand to her arm. His touch has flashed her elsewhere: *When is this? Howard and I newly divorced. Dani has come out to us, separately, on the phone. Climactically to me, as I'd known that she was still contemplating her orientation. Out of the blue to her father. And now we three are together for the first time since all that. For lunch at the Hard Rock Café in Chicago. The first moments. His hand on Dani's arm. Warm words. And his following embrace of her. Yes. An act simply of the mind or not, he was fine with her about her identity. He was utterly convincing. From the beginning and ever since. If willed, at least his position was based on appropriate thoughts.*

He withdraws his hand from her arm. He has apparently finished whatever it was he had to say. She is conscious of it being about her story last night. Something about parts interrogating other parts. And he was approving of it.

She has a quick decision to make. Let him know she wasn't listening and ask him to repeat it. Or not actually care about what he had to say and keep on moving.

"Thanks so much for that," she says. "I don't want to interrupt your writing. Get back to work now. Me too."

And she passes into the bedroom, thinking: *It makes no difference. That story was for me.*

☞

"So you still haven't slept?" Amanda asks that evening, sitting before Howard as he opens his MacBook on his lap.

"Since I can't remember when," he says.

"Welcome to the club."

"I will strive for coherence."

"I make no demands in that regard," she says. "I have no expectations."

"Nor do you have any confidence, it sounds like."

"Wrong. I meant that sweetly."

"Sorry. I meant that wryly."

"It sounds like we should begin."

And Howard reads.

ৡৡ

THE FOURTH TALE
Howard

A bar in New Haven with a massive mirror.

A place where you drink and at the same time are forced to see yourself any time you glance up. Or worse than anytime. Unceasingly. Unremittingly. You can't stop looking at the idiot. It seemed that bad a year after meeting a swell girl in Paris with a swell body and a swell mind, not necessarily in that order—not in that order, at all, really, a swell mind first that made the body even better—then circumstances ended what you began, ended it unavoidably, given where you were (Yale) and where she was (WashU, St. Louis) and where your minds and ambitions were. Hers drifting in an unfocused semi-artsy way. Yours dealing with a senior year in comparative literature and applying to graduate schools and hoping that student deferments last and you don't end up instead in a body bag heading home from Vietnam. So the Paris romance, as fine as it was, could not realistically continue. It wasn't meant to be. But still. But fucking still.

And so I was looking at myself nonstop while I drank in a bar, at age twenty-one unimpeded at last. A neo-denizen. And it felt like unimpeded was way too much of both, on this particular evening. Both the drinking and me.

So I started nursing the beer in front of me.

And it happened that there was a girl sitting nearby at the bar.

This being what I was inclined to call them back then. *Girl*, which was even what I'd occasionally called the young woman who I'd thought was so very swell in Paris. In fact, I already *have* called her that, 236 words ago. Which puts this rhetorical tic in perspective, surely.

So about the girl sitting near me.

She had a strong jaw. With eyes that could've been blue

or they could've been gray, but in the light of a bar, who the hell would ever have known which. Probably blue, was my second thought. Gray is rare, I thought, compulsively continuing the close read of her face even, as a unified whole, that face was very appealing and she was looking at me. But the jaw was the thing. It was strong enough that its accompanying mouth would be capable of telling me to stop being a fucking idiot and forget what I've already screwed up and say something to her.

"Hello," I said.

"Hello," she said.

"I'm Howard."

"I'm Judith."

"I'm at Yale."

"I'm at the Peaches and Cream Beauty Salon."

This stopped me.

"That stopped you," she said.

"No," I said.

"Yes," she said.

"Yes, I said. "But not yes in the way you think. I confronted my own assumption. Though I hasten to add the assumption included not a scintilla—not a tiny bit—of class prejudice."

"You sure?"

"About the prejudice? Yes."

"Isn't that why you defined *scintilla* for me?"

This was a rhetorical question. Rightly so. But she smiled with seeming unsarcastic sweetness as she said it.

I confessed. "Well, maybe a scintilla of why. I'm sorry."

"I'll give you a pass," she said.

"Can we start this again?" I said.

"I'm Judith."

"I'm Howard."

"I work at the Peaches and Cream Beauty Salon," she said.

For whatever dumb-shit reason, this stopped me once more. For a mere fragment of a moment.

But long enough for her to jump in. "Starting over doesn't change who we are," she said.

"Of course not."

"I have to be frank," she said.

"Please."

"These clouds around us should have begun to clear by now."

"Are there clouds?"

"If you listen close."

"I regret my part in that," I said. I meant it.

She nodded. She took a sip of her beer. Its color was near to the color of her hair, a muted gold. A pilsner, no doubt. It struck me that she liked her beer the way she seemed to like her conversation, a little bitter. It occurred to me to say as much. But that wouldn't sound clever. It would sound sarcastic. So I did not say as much. Then it struck me that I liked this young woman. This not-girl.

I sipped my own beer.

She was looking at me when I turned her way again.

"So what do you study?" she said.

"Comparative literature. English Department."

"Where everyone learns to *scintilla*," she said.

I didn't mean to flinch faintly at this. She'd earned the dig. I even kind of liked the dig.

But she said, "Sorry." And then, "My father does this. Banters the snot out of you."

"It's okay," I said.

"You just pick it up."

"What does he do? For a living."

"He's an auto mechanic. Owns his own shop."

I had absolutely no idea what to say about that.

Perhaps sensing I was already snotless, she helped me out. "He banters in his own way."

I cast about for a follow-up question or observation. Something perhaps about car dealers' mechanics versus independents. But nothing coherent was coming to mind.

So in the meantime I offered a lame "Good."

To her credit, she let me further off the hook. "What does *your* father do?"

"Pushes paper and bosses people," I said.

"Anything on those papers?"

"Insurance business," I said.

"Deaths and fires and such?"

"Mostly."

"Does he have a boss?"

I heard her saying: *Unlike my father.*

"Up a couple of floors."

"I bet your father's important there."

"Yes," I said. "As a matter of fact, he is. Or should I say *incidentally* he is."

"'Matter of fact' does it," she said.

We both fell silent for a few moments.

Then she said, "So do you really want to be here?"

"Drinking in this bar?"

"Yale," she said. "Instead of joining your daddy's firm?"

"Hell yes."

"Because it keeps you out of Vietnam?"

Once again she stopped me.

Her tone was a tone crafted for a privileged son of a

bitch who was gaming a corrupt system.

She was watching me closely. Reading my face.

And I was reading hers. A close read. Like a modernist text.

This wasn't banter. This was the subtext of all we'd said. This was the theme.

I said, "All the boys you know are getting drafted."

"As a matter of fact," she said.

"I'm not going to apologize."

"I didn't expect you to."

"There are a lot of Yalies in this joint," I said. "My impression is you're as smart as any of us. So is this a true, felt sadness for the draftees or are we sport for you? That you come here to wrestle with us."

She looked away.

She drained the last two fingers of her beer.

"Can I buy you another?" I asked.

She looked at me and then at her empty glass. She was thinking this over. And then she stepped down from her bar stool.

"Thanks," she said. "But no."

"Too bad," I said.

"Really," she said. "You're cute. Got a brain. Too bad you're clean under the fingernails."

And she turned and walked away.

Out the door.

I haunted that bar. Till the day I graduated and my hometown draft board cancelled university deferments and I was grabbed up into the Army and I ended up in Vietnam, till then I haunted that bar.

But I never saw her again.

꙳

Howard's MacBook snaps shut.

He feels pretty good about the writing. He feels pretty good about where it came from in him. Given those feelings, however, he's *not* feeling good about the blankness of Amanda's face.

Behind the façade Amanda is struggling. This feels a little creepy to her. She wants to challenge him but she wants to keep it civil. She works hard to speak calmly. She says, "Did my having a past connection with someone make you feel threatened by my memory of it?"

"Pardon me?"

"I tell you about Kathleen and it agitates you, so you change your plans and stay up all night to write your regret at losing a chance for love with Judith."

"It never occurred to me."

"Really?"

"Not as payback," he says. "Not as argument. I'm just trying to follow what you've always advocated in print about what you do. Dip into what I've forgotten. Into my unconscious. That goes for great personal essays too, doesn't it? Retrieve the memory instead of twist it."

Through this little rejoinder, Amanda processes his words: *He's correct. It's how I write. It's why he's suddenly showing a talent at this.*

Nevertheless. Based on another truth of her writing process, she says, still with assiduous calmness, affecting, indeed, his own scholarly tone, "But where—in this particular context—did you choose to dip? A tale of the road not taken."

That last bit has been said not quite so calmly.

He shrugs.

A shrug? Yes. Which her still sharper tone now duly notes: "Kathleen could never have happened. But it certainly sounds like your Judith could've."

Howard sucks a noisy breath of indignation and rises. "She was never *my* Judith."

"Not for want of haunting." This she says—to her surprise—calmly again, with something like sadness.

Howard has no reply. He rises and moves off toward the balcony.

They both have heard the taint of retrospective jealousy in her. He has a flash of recognition at the irritation his own such reactions have caused. Her flash is that it is not just a quirk of Howard's. Or simply a trait of men.

He steps onto the balcony, leans into the railing and the dark. But there is no solace here. In the distance is the high-tone low-tone, high-tone low-tone wail of an ambulance. And off to the right and down below, the French couple are at it again.

He feels only exhaustion.

He turns and moves quietly past Amanda and into the bedroom.

◌◌

By the time Amanda has a glass of wine, and mulls the evening to no conclusion whatsoever, and does a couple of dishes, and enters the bedroom hoping there's no more talk tonight, Howard is fast asleep in his pajamas but with his covers only partly folded upon him. Not his way of sleeping.

She is reminded that he spent most of the past night awake working on his story.

She gently pulls the covers fully over him.

The room is chilly.

March 23, 2020

After eating her breakfast alone, Amanda goes to the window and sits. She ponders that moment just before bed last night. The moment when her hand found its way to the quilt to draw it over the sleeping Howard. She'd had a difficult twenty-four hours with him. But her right hand decided to let that go. Decided to be gentle. And the impulse lingers now in her writerly fingertips. Which suggests an appropriate alternate story for this night. Amanda and Howard agreed before this trip to make a serious effort to rip up—or at least archive—their lists of disaffection with each other for the sake of Paris.

"All right," she says, softly.

She will rewrite another tale on the day of its deadline.

It's already a sunlit morning, but she's confident that the twelve or so hours before her will be adequate.

CR

It turns out she needed all of those hours, and now it's time to read to Howard without a proper last proofing read to herself.

So the ritual reigns: Amanda and Howard sit and they face each other and the MacBook of the night comes to its owner's lap and the lid rises and it shines a light on the face of the reader. At this point the listener is allowed to initiate a brief dialog with the reader.

On this night, Howard says, "You've worked furiously all day."

"Yet another change of story."

"A change?"

"Yes."

"A change." A thump of a repetition.

She hears a hint of suspicion in this.

"Inspiration," she says.

"Of course," he says.

And she thinks: *He's expecting a lost love of my own.*

And he thinks: *Christ almighty. Is it to be a lost love of her own?*

Amanda pauses to consider what she is about to read: *Oh shit.* For this one particular reader before her, the first couple of pages could well be misunderstood.

"You are a professional reader, of sorts," she says. "May I appeal to that professionalism and ask you not to jump to any conclusions in the first few hundred words?"

Howard ungrits his teeth. "I am. You may. I will not."

There is a moment of silence between them.
He appends, "Will not jump."
"Thank you," she says.
And she begins to read.

‽‽

THE FIFTH TALE
Amanda

When I first saw him, I thought Chekhov. I thought
Lenin. I thought of Anthony Van Dyke himself. The
prompt having been a somewhat pointed beard and an
unassumingly overarching mustache, but all these references being a little vague, being from memory, being
the process that happened in a flash as I stepped inside
the legendary, floor-to-ceiling, nooked-and-crannied,
labyrinthine English language bookshop in the Rue de la
Bûcherie in Paris. Shakespeare and Company. And the
whiskers belonged to the owner and creator, George
Whitman. I was here to sit for an hour and sign my books.

He greeted me within my first few steps into the
cramped, book-besotted front room. "Amanda Duval,"
he said. His voice was warm. His next words were, "You
are precise," even though I'd been due at 4:00 p.m.
and it was now 4:05 p.m. But his voice remained warm.
Seemingly devoid of irony. In spite of my arriving too late
to justify that bit of praise from the most famous independent bookseller in the literary world, a man who, not incidentally, was equally famous for his crankiness. Though
I'd given him reason to justifiably display that latter trait,
he did not.

79

He even patted me on the arm.

But he then did turn his back on me and stride away. I followed, and in the next comparably book-bedecked room, a dozen people stood waiting for me before a wooden table where sat a triple stack of *The One He Never Spoke Of* by Amanda Duval. A first novel. About Ernest Hemingway's Paris lover who remained a secret, even from future biographers. Mainly because I created her for the book. And made her the protagonist. I had struggled with my publisher, not so much my editor, who joined me in my plea—as dead men can't sue for libel— but the publisher's lawyers, who ultimately prevailed in having me pseudonymize Hemingway's name to avoid problems with his estate. Mary Welsh was still very much alive, after all. Not that there was any doubt who the writer was. And the change did, I must admit, allow me the enjoyment of inventing Papa-like book titles and passages, resisting any impulse toward parody. My book was about two lovers, one of whom was not allowed her full identity outside of the hidden relationship with a famous man. All of which, for 1976, was fresh and worthy of off-the-book-page coverage, where the model for the fictional character could be openly discussed. It certainly was the reason I found myself at a wobbly wooden table in an inner room of Shakespeare and Company in Paris for a first-novel book signing.

Which, in turn, was arguably the only reason I ended up getting a chance to marry Howard Blevins.

So I received half an hour of steady customers, half a dozen of whom needed my confirmation that yes, the writer in the book is actually based on Ernest Hemingway, but no, the previously unknown Hemingway lover is made up, and one of whom, a Frenchman pedantically fluent in English, needed to argue with me about my ending the book's title in a preposition.

And then I looked up for the next customer and found him standing before me. Eight years later.

"Howard," I said, in a tone that was flat but merely from shock.

"Amanda," he said in a tone that was warm, his having had time ahead to absorb the situation and manage his tone.

"May we start again?" I asked. A bit plaintive.

"Start?" Flat himself now.

I meant the tone. The declaration of names. His own flatness suggested that he'd thought I meant our affair. I said, "I simply wanted to say *Howard* once again. With the warmth you gave my name. You took me by surprise."

"Feel free," he said.

"Howard," I said, quite warmly. Quite.

"Amanda," he said. Quite warmly.

Meanwhile we have both of us been ignoring the presence of three or four actual customers waiting behind him for me to sign their books. People with ears to hear. People, indeed, who were enraptured with the little scene playing before them as if from one of the books that looked upon us all from floor to ceiling in all directions.

So Howard opened his copy of *The One He Never Spoke Of* and laid it before me.

He'd chosen the half-title page, with its abundant white space.

I took up my pen.

I wrote: "For Howard."

Oh shit, I thought. *What the hell to say. Should I write with irony? That is, very formally, as if he were simply the next person in this line? Should I write my heart? As I feel it flailing around in my chest? Or something in between? But what the hell would in-between be?*

No, I advised myself. *Just enter your writing Zone. Just put the pen to the paper and let 'er rip.*

Which I did. I wrote: "How the hell did you find me? After eight years? In another country? And why? Not that any of that matters. Except for the why. I'm glad. Whatever this all turns out to mean."

Got it all in. With a separate line left over for a signature. Which, after only the briefest of pauses, I signed with bookstore-signing formality: "Amanda Duval."

I shut the cover, rather authoritatively. His attempts to read the inscription upside down while standing over me as I wrote it had clearly been unsuccessful.

"See you after?" I asked.

"Yes," he said.

So he moved off, and after reading my inscription, he floated along the walls. Looking at books. His back to me. From the glances his way I was able to steal, he might as well have been an utter stranger. Eight years ago, when we'd left the Sorbonne and returned to the States, we'd both recognized that it would be impossible to maintain our relationship. In practical terms. And more: It had to be all the way serious for us or not at all.

We were twenty-one.

And we were separately ambitious.

Very.

So we'd kissed goodbye, with every reason to think it was forever.

And we vanished from each other.

Till that late afternoon in Paris when I smiled and chatted and signed at Shakespeare and Company for what felt like a much longer time than it probably was while Howard Blevins of all people lingered nearby.

Then there was a lull, and George Whitman promptly appeared.

I thanked him.

He thanked me.

Ten minutes later Howard and I were sitting on the river-edge parapet along the Promenade Maurice Carême. We dangled our feet over the Seine. Our backs were to the high retaining wall, and the Cathédrale Notre-Dame de Paris was immediately beyond. We'd chosen to flirt with the river while facing Shakespeare and Company on the other side. Though the shop wasn't quite visible from where we sat, it was enough to know it was there.

On that opposite quay a woman in a long dark coat with a hood was feeding the river birds.

Howard and I fell silent.

A silence which lingered. And which seemed fine. And along the way I'm not sure which of us moved—it didn't take much, and it might have been both of us collaborating unawares—but I suddenly realized that our shoulders and upper arms were now touching as we sat.

Finally Howard said, "Were we always this contented together in silence?"

"Were we ever silent?" I said.

Howard laughed softly. "We did fill the air."

"Perhaps *she's* the reason. For our silence." I nodded to the woman across the river. She was still there. The black figure against the gray wall, the begging birds in the air and along the bank, though she was motionless now.

"She's the test," Howard said. "Not the reason. Seems to me."

I looked at him. He was right. In our past life together we would have started talking about her as soon as we'd seen her.

I looked back to our woman. I gently baited him: "She's put us in our bodies by the Seine. The dark uprightness of her, unbending even as she throws her fragments of bread. The herring gulls and Duclair ducks wheeling and circling. And the Seine flowing, the green of twilight-darkened bookstalls."

I continued to watch the woman I'd just evoked.

Howard remained silent.

He was processing all this in his own way. I knew the words forming in him would be of a fundamentally different sort from mine. Which was why we had always filled the air.

But he was taking long enough to speak that I prodded some more.

I said, "Contented by way of our bodies, yes? The senses. What we perceive and imaginatively share through them." At this I nodded toward woman and birds and river. Then I translated this a bit for the scholar whose shoulder and arm have lain against mine for a long while now: "Contented by the color, the movement. The smell and the shape. The thereness of things."

And Howard said, "Actually, watching our bird-feeding woman in black, Tolstoy's methods come to mind. That wonderful scene in *Anna Karenina*, for instance. That fateful great ball when Vronsky and Anna meet and begin to dance onward to their fates. She wears black. The color of death. Even as all around her are women in lilac, a color of the engorged bloom of ardent growth, the color of the season among the Russian aristocracy. The color of transient life. But she wears the color of death itself. For her. For the man who approaches her. And it wins him. She is beautiful in black. And it foresees the death of them both."

He paused. He smiled at me.

He added, "Contented by way of our minds, yes? What we uniquely comprehend and explicate through them. The thought, the literary form, the mimesis and the symbolism and the theme, the critical analysis of things."

Howard and I looked at each other. I, of course, saw the avid connectedness of his eyes on me. Surely he saw the same—which I knew to be there—in my eyes on him. Surely *that* wasn't cause for instant, distancing analysis.

But without taking his eyes off me, he nodded his head sideways toward the quay across the way and said, "We know more about birds than they do about themselves."

I smiled at him. I wondered if he knew how to interpret the smile. Ironically? That I understood the point he was making even as I devalued it? Or without irony? I should accept that artists need literary criticism or they won't even know what they're saying? Please.

I let the smile go. Even as I found myself, a little to my surprise, actually enjoying this give and take with my overthoughtful, once and future lover. And I said, "But what we know that the birds don't is irrelevant to them. What *they* know that we *don't* is how to fly. What that feels like. To spread our arms and lift away from the earth and fly. The closest we can ever get to that is for the literary artist to imagine the experience profoundly and to write of it directly, to our otherwise earthbound bodies. So that we might inhabit a bird through art."

And at this, Howard Blevins, in what I felt at the time to be a smart bit of close-reading, took me into his arms and kissed me.

A long kiss.

And when it ended and we pulled apart just a bit, I said to him, "So you agree."

And he said, "I can't say that I do. But you made your case persuasively."

⧼⧽

The end. Amanda snaps her computer sharply shut. More sharply than she intends. Sharply enough that she hears how the gesture could be heard as somehow angry.

Which isn't what she seems to be feeling forty-three years later. She even wonders: *Do we kiss right now, in real life? In a way we have not kissed for a long while?*

But she abruptly doubts it.

She still has not looked at him.

She is looking at her hand that snapped the computer lid. Does that hand understand more than her brain about what she's presently feeling? Or even more than her heart? More now than it knew rearranging the covers last night?

Her remembrance of the actual kiss that has raised these questions suddenly has a whiff of sentimentality about it.

But no. It's something else. Something worse. It is beyond the sentimental. Beyond the spirit of the tale she ended up writing.

She needed that final proofing read, needed to free herself

from the temporality of last night's gesture.

The last line—his words just after that kiss—are precisely the words he spoke in life. They will remain. But what presently follows is false.

She finally looks Howard in the face.

He's staring at her. Not unfriendly. Not unappreciative. Meditative. As if he were—literary scholar that he is—preparing to enumerate the themes she has manifested. As an act of pedagogical respect. Enumerate them as if each abstract word was itself the experience of it.

He immediately confirms her impression: "Ah," he says. "The themes of Amanda Duval."

She raises her hand to stop him. "Now that you've invoked themes," she says, "I realize I have to rewrite the ending."

Howard smiles footnotedly and quotes, "The only kind of writing is rewriting."

"Something like that."

"You want to go back to the bedroom?"

"I can do it here," she says. "This replaces everything beginning with the kiss."

She steadies the MacBook on her thighs, banishes Howard's very presence from her mind, wanting these next words to come from the right place in her. Ad hominem being just as wrongheaded as thematic ideation.

She blocks and deletes the last four paragraphs of her story.

She is ready, resolving to create not from spite but from honesty, both personal and artistic.

Over the next ten minutes she improvises a replacement. Tweaks it here and there. Saves it and sits back.

She finds Howard's eyes fixed on her.

And she reads to him:

"At this, Howard Blevins, in what I briefly misinterpreted to be a bit of close-reading, took me into his arms and kissed me.

When it ended and we pulled apart, I said to him, 'So you agree.'

And he said, 'I can't say that I do. But you made your case persuasively.'

He smiled, as if I were to understand this paradox as charming.

In fact, in that moment, I understood that it was not paradox at all. He was patronizing me.

He granted me the illusion of persuasion but only to a lesser mind than his, as he'd made clear from the outset that he was not persuaded.

I heard it. I knew it.

And he had thus spoiled the kiss.

There would be *un*spoiled kisses, as well, in the years to come. Many of them. Even in that night to come.

But upon that first, reuniting kiss—and inevitably, comparably, upon many subsequent kisses—there was a taint."

For Howard, it's not that this sentiment is all that new between them. He suspects of most literary scholars—as of himself—that if they were to deeply examine their quest for self, which Amanda privileges, they would admit that what they do is not infrequently a patronizing pat, a patronizing squeeze on the author's shoulder. Many scholars wouldn't even have to look all that deep. But Howard also absolutely insists: Respect and patronage can coexist. Can even embrace. And yes, can even fuck their mutual brains out, which he hazily recalls is how the story of that particular evening recounted in Amanda's tale actually ended.

Not that he will make this argument to his wife at the moment.

Not that he doesn't regret their reuniting kiss more than four decades ago having apparently been spoiled for her. Which he also does not say, not willing to accept the blame.

All this has reasoned and proclaimed its way around inside Howard's mind while outwardly he has remained inert.

He remains so even still.

Which is okay with Amanda for now, his seeming lack of affect. It is sufficient that he is not taking up the fight.

She is weary.

And she is aware of the paradox: She rewrote the end of her story to discard its sentimentality, but to whine about the tone of a particular kiss is to sentimentalize it. She vaguely remembers that subsequent evening having gone quite well.

But still. She wishes the run of twelve hours leading up to her reading had yielded those last few changes ahead of time.

Considering where she and Howard are and why, it still feels like a point worth making.

Husband and wife stare at each other for another moment.

Then Howard says, "And so to bed."

Amanda clamps down on her impulse to challenge her oblivious husband over a lapse of scholarly perception: To benignly and literately end this evening, Howard has quoted Samuel Pepys famously in the act of closing his diary, pulling up his covers, and blowing out his candle, even though it is now widely known that Pepys often did so after still another day of sexual predation in that bed, even unto pedophilia.

But that's a tangential point tonight.

She keeps quiet.

Howard rises.

She waits for him to pass.

As he does, he slows and puts his hand on Amanda's shoulder. By reflex he gently pats her there and ends the pat with an equally gentle squeeze.

He has already taken a step away, and another, out of earshot, when she quietly observes: "Motherfuck."

But Amanda's silent elaboration on that is—in all fairness— to and about herself. *Unless you're ready to just end it all in the morning, fess up. For years you've knowingly patted Howard in just that way. A man you have meanwhile married twice. Respect and patronage can coexist.*

March 24, 2020

On the next morning Howard rises first. When Amanda wakes, he is standing at their balcony, fully dressed.

They both have slept fully.

She puts on her dressing gown and steps out beside him.

She stands near, but their arms do not touch.

Their voices, however, are gentle in their first words of the day, as he says "Good morning" and she says "Good morning" and she leans forward with her hips against the railing.

"Can I make you some coffee?" he says.

"A little later perhaps. This is nice right now." She nods at the empty park below them.

"Yes," he says.

He is leaning uprightly as well. He's been sightlessly residing as far off as he can from where he stands, out at the Butte Montmartre and the spires of Sacré-Coeur. This is his on-deadline writing day. Having offered Amanda coffee, he returns to his sighted place, which is inward, which is distant from this balcony by half a century and half a world. His tale underway has set itself in Vietnam.

Amanda's gaze has gone to the California sequoia, its narrow-shouldered upper body rising above the matronly topped Continental trees. When Amanda and Howard first met as young twenty-somethings in this park, the sequoia had recently turned a hundred years old. So it is a hundred and fiftyish now. Sequoias live three thousand years.

"What the hell tale does that French park and its near-eternal California tree think it's trying to tell?" Amanda asks. Not just asks. She *demands*, taking a half step back from the railing. "It doesn't even require a close read to get it. Human life is but a fleeting terminal disease. Is what."

"Not sure where that came from," Howard says. "But I think you need that coffee now."

"You're probably right."

"I've got you covered," he says.

He goes.

Amanda takes the half-step return to the balcony edge. She leans there once more.

She shifts her eyes from the sequoia to the Temple de la Sybille and its eight Corinthian columns.

But she too looks inward.

She must begin to write for tomorrow.

She's got nothing.

She thinks: *Perhaps the park is right about literary inspiration, as well. It's fleeting. It's terminal. Perhaps, at age seventy-two, I knew three more brief tales to tell and that was that.*

Amanda drifts in the mid-ocean wake of that thought until Howard says, from behind her, "I thought you'd want to go two-fisted this morning."

She turns to him, noting the lightness of his voice, and indeed, he has poured her coffee into one of their French coffee bowls for two-handed breakfast drinking. She thinks what a healing thing his patronizing pat on her shoulder must have been for him last night. And she thinks yet again this morning that it is true for both of them, that to patronize is perhaps more often an act of self-healing than self-superiority.

"Thank you," she says, taking the bowl with her two hands, but pausing before her first sip. "You've had yours?" she asks.

"Yes." His voice is flat.

"You don't like the French coffee."

"I've tried to keep that terrible secret from you."

"I know you too well," she says.

"I do miss the delicately roasted fruit-forward notes of my Ethiopian-sourced pour-overs."

"That's the man I know."

"And married," he says.

"And married," she says.

In this last little two-word exchange they both worked hard not to sound sarcastic in tone. He managed nostalgic. She managed wistful.

Twice, they both add now, just to themselves, a little bit baffled, for the moment, at all the struggle.

Amanda takes her first sip of coffee.

Something stirs in her.

"You're right," she says. "About wanting to do it with two fists. Even from vaguely sourced Robusta beans dark-roasted to the brink of burnt."

He stifles a chuckle, keeps a straight face, thinking, *She's right about her taste in coffee*. "I'm happy you're happy," he says.

He means it. *That's the woman I know.*

And she realizes now that the stirring in her was not to the prospect of caffeine. It was to felt inspiration.

She is moved to say, "Can we try to let go of the past three nights?"

"Yes," he says. "Whatever we're up to, let's reboot."

"You just brought me my story for tomorrow in a ceramic bowl."

"And so to work," he says.

"And so to work," she says.

❧

The evening comes, and even when the words have grown elusive or resistant, the writing itself has felt good to each of them. The reason is simple and well known to Amanda: They have been writing every day. For a week now. Every day.

They sit before each other.

And for the first time since he chose to turn to it, he reveals to her, "I've written about Vietnam."

"Howard," she says, the only word she can think to speak at this announcement. She hears her own tone, wishing it to be supportive. Admiring even. But she hears it only as surprised.

She musters her warmth, which she legitimately feels. "How fine," she says.

After their decades together, Amanda knows only the minimum about that year of his life. He has made it clear that his reticence is not because of the horrors of war but because of what struck him as a kind of touristic mundanity about his encounter with it. He was a noncombatant support soldier, true of the vast majority of all the soldiers in all modern wars. He was implanted without the language in an exotic corner of the world that had no accessible literary history to engage him. He was quartered in a former French colonial hotel in Saigon, a city which remained relatively calm—by the standards of that war—for the full year he was there. And his own personal assignment, based on the Army actually noting his education and training him accordingly, resulted in his composing speeches and correspondence for a MACV general and then for a US foreign service officer at Saigon City Hall.

In spite of his having made all this emphatically but summarily clear to Amanda, she has nevertheless always suspected that there had been far more than that to his experience in Vietnam.

Indeed, as he now faces her on this night, he says, "I've been listening to you. My body was there. I was in my body in Vietnam. The stuff of tales, yes? Even true ones."

"Yes," she says.

And he begins.

৵৽৶

THE SIXTH TALE
Howard

She was probably a bar girl. Which was to say, in Saigon in 1970, a prostitute. Probably a bar girl even if the bar was well off Tự Do Street, where American servicemen traditionally sought their *short-time girls*. It was obvious I was simply privately seeking a beer, but the young woman instantly shifted her stool choice from one end of the bar to the other, arriving to sit beside me. And she struck up a conversation in pretty good but GI-inflected English that undermined her attempts to distance herself from the taint of Tự Do. Eventually she even worked around to wistfully whisper, "I hope someday find number-one man I love long-time."

And maybe that was true. She was dressed the way the young women of Saigon dressed up nice—the young women you take home forever—in the traditional *áo dài*, a dress with a tight-fitting bodice and long panels front and back from waist to toes, with billowy black silk pants beneath.

Howard interrupts his own tale.

He pulls back from his computer screen, willing himself to look Amanda in the eyes.

He has just heard himself.

And he addresses what he strongly suspects she is thinking in one form or another. "No," he says. "This is not another two roads diverging in a yellow wood. I'm not even going to whisk her away for an evening or turn her into an exotic temporary girlfriend or even simply turn wistful myself. I didn't hear how this would sound till just now. How far it is from what I'm getting at."

Amanda says, "My problem—which I admit is nagging at me yet again—is a result of two stories in a row, Howie. Even after our circumspection last night."

"I understand."

"From half a century ago, two bars on two sides of the world with two young women drawn to you for a two-step dance of self-revelation."

"Let me go on, Mandy. The story's out of whack in its emphasis so far, but you'll see."

"I wasn't the one who stopped you. I was assiduously biting my tongue."

"I know. Thank you."

Howard finds himself a little breathless now.

He hesitates.

Not for long.

Amanda says, "So get on with it."

And he does.

He searches his screen for what's next.

"Do *not* back up," Amanda says.

He nods. Once. Sharply.

And his intent is to resume.

But he sees the words up ahead. In them he will soon record his conversation with this likely short-timer bargirl as she aspires to find love and permanence with a man who might transport her away from this world at war. And he flirts with her just a little bit, asking her to teach him a Vietnamese phrase for "very beautiful." One that he can use for a sunset or a woman. Anything in Vietnam that is beautiful. And yes. Flirts a little, even adding, "A phrase I can use for a young Saigon woman wearing an *áo dài* in a bar and longing for a better future." Not that the comment will lead anywhere. Not in the selectivity of this telling of it. But not even in life. It led nowhere that should make his wife, who sits before him, uncomfortable. Should. Ha. He's playing by their rules emphasizing the truth. But that doesn't mean he has to put in everything he can remember.

He resumes reading. But he jump cuts, and he edits out a bit more on the fly:

Whatever were her longings and however she might have shifted her seat at the bar in possible pursuit of them, we small-talked our way through the end of my beer and then, before I slipped away, I thought to ask her a question the like of which I had routinely asked other bilingual Vietnamese I'd encountered. "I greatly regret not having trained in your language before coming here," I said. "So I sometimes ask for a phrase. Can you teach me some brief phrase that will be useful in Saigon?"

She straightened a bit and smiled a small, faintly lop-sided smile. "Đẹp quá," she said. And she repeated it carefully, exaggerating the phonetics, making me repeat each word separately till I knew them. *Dap*. But forced down into my throat at its speaking, a glottal tone in this tonal language. And *kwah*. With a rising tone.

I had learned how to hear the tones in Vietnamese pretty clearly.

I mastered these two words quickly.

She laughed.

"Say it," she said. "Two words same time."

"Đẹp quá," I said.

"Number one," she said.

And I asked, "All right. What does that mean?"

"Very beautiful," she said.

"To say this about what?"

"Say it any time," she said. "The moon go up. See a beautiful woman. Same same."

"Very useful," I said. "Thank you."

And I said goodbye.

I went out into the street.

The sun was setting. I was in civilian clothes—an ongoing perk of my job at Saigon City Hall—and I liked to walk the city at this time of day. I'd come not just to accept but to embrace the wild dislocation that had over-taken my life. Eventually I would understand this impulse as having flowed from the same place in me as my impulse to move through the dusky streets of a literary writer's text, a writer's subtext, a writer's life and way of thinking and way of analyzing the world, move, as well, through the ways of other scholars as they wandered the same streets as I.

I felt these streets in Saigon were my own. I passed the Caravelle Hotel, still catering to civilians with a doorman in hotel livery and a rifle slung over his shoulder. And I paused at a bookstall, just closing. My eyes fell to literary names on Vietnamese paperbacks in a uniform paperbound edition: Rilke. Henry Miller. Nietzsche, whose Vietnamese title—*Tôi là Ai?*—I could make out into English: *Who Am I?* And in the same series *Antony và Cleopatra* with Shakespeare's face visible in the top half of the cover but with a paper wrapper below proclaiming him as a winner of the Nobel Prize.

I walked on, resisting the urge to fantasize about the Bard walking across the stage at the Stockholm Concert Hall in lace collar, padded doublet, knee breeches, and with a rosette upon his instep to receive his Nobel Prize, instead letting that revelation of the Vietnamese publisher clear my head of the hotel bar and open me to what had become my frequent evening tryst with Saigon.

At the next corner I turned toward the river, moving beneath the densely canopied tamarind trees first brought to Vietnam by the French navy a hundred years ago. Ahead was the long run of Tự Do Street bars, and I did unfurl one last thought of the girl who taught me this day's bit of Vietnamese, a thought of her longing for escape, and I realized I never even asked her name.

And then I stepped to the curb and hailed a motorized xích-lô, a ubiquitous Vietnamese equivalent of the Chinese rickshaw but with a thrilling difference. Instead of sitting behind a laboriously pedaling taximan, the passenger sits on an open bench in front of the driver of a two-stroke engine. The ride is fast and buffeting, with nothing at all of the machine in your field of vision. Instead is the brisk run of the street and its colonial shopfronts and balconies and its tamarind trees and its chestnut and its resin trees, and as I leaned into the rush of things my sense of speed shifted from my cheeks and the back of my head and suddenly, ecstatically, into my chest, into the very center of my chest.

I flew headlong down Trần Hưng Đạo street and I had a flicker of regret at the eventual sight ahead of the Metropole, my hotel. Part of me wanted to rush onward. But a familiar, slower, more personal pleasure awaited, and my hotel was the starting place when night came on.

I paid the driver and descended at the Metropole's front door.

Across the street our own two short-timer joints—the Okay Lounge and the San Francisco Bar—were starting up their evening trade. One of them had its jukebox cranked up with the Stones' "Honky Tonk Women."

I nodded at the South Vietnamese soldier who guarded our hotel front door. He'd taught me how to say the equivalent of *Good evening, pal*, and I'd taught him that same phrase in English. Since no one was around, we exchanged that mutual greeting. He'd also taught me, at my request, the simplest way to say that I was going for a walk. Which I said now. "Tôi đang đi dạo."

He smiled and even tilted his head slightly in the direction he knew I'd take.

Which I did, along west on Trần Hưng Đạo.

I sauntered. The last light of day would soon be gone. I liked the fresh blackness of night where I was going.

At last I crossed the boulevard and entered the vast warren of alleyways between Trần Hưng Đạo and the Bến Nghé canal. The narrow passages were dominated by, defined by, the matrix of the dark, but that gave each cubbyhole of home or shop a bulb-lit or candle-lit or paraffin-lit singularity. And I was known by now to many of the residents. Known to walk their narrow passageways, known well-enough for them to continue their lives as if unaware of me, which was a fine thing to my mind, my accepted presence here, and sometimes they smiled and nodded and I spoke a few of their words to them with the tones just right.

But I kept moving.

They understood.

Often as I passed, they would, unawares, gift me with the sight of the gestures of their private lives: A woman pushes a lock of her long hair back from her face. A man opens a newspaper. A mother is coining away the symptoms of some sickness from her teenage daughter—perhaps a headache, a cold, nausea—a century-old therapy of rubbing a coin on the back or neck or head, rubbing unto bruising, the therapy known in Vietnamese as *cạo gió*, "to scrub the wind."

And all around were the smells of this densely humanized neighborhood half a planet away from my home, smells of incense and wood fire and grease and kerosene and fish sauce—my Saigon's famous *nước mắm*—and yes, as well, the smells of rot and of garbage and of piss. All colliding and separating and supplanting and blending. The blend being olfactory but also being a deep emotional impression: that here was human life lived intensely and intimately, in the middle of a war.

And on this particular night I had the impulse to stop, in the dark, before a small room, open to the alley and lit in its center by a hanging incandescent bulb.

She was young. Very thin. A mother, sitting there in the light. She held her child on her lap, the child small enough—possibly diminished or stunted enough—that I could not guess its age, though young enough that perhaps the mother had just now finished feeding it from her breast. The child wore a dingy infant T-shirt.

The mother looked at me.

I realized I knew what to say.

The mother was unmoving, unflinching in her gaze.

Of course.

I was an American. A dumb-shit American.

But her expectation was minimal. She would forgive me if I made an error.

So I extended my hand, turning the palm upward as I did, inclining my head as well, clearly pointing to her baby.

And I said, "Đẹp quá."

The mother smiled.

Slowly she bowed her face to me, in respect.

I bowed mine to her, just as slowly.

Then the mother turned and bent to her baby and kissed it on the forehead. On my behalf, I felt.

I walked on, into the night. I thought again of the nameless young woman in the bar, and my mind made her the sister of the nameless young woman with her baby, the two of them having taken different but equally brutal paths in a country that had been at war for as long as they could remember, moving away from what they felt was nearly nothing toward what they desperately hoped was something.

☙❧

After a minimal beat of silence to acknowledge the tale's end, Amanda says, "I'm sorry for needing to bite my tongue about the bar and the girl. My assuming you had the same agenda in Saigon as you did in New Haven. And I know that sounds like more suspicion, or criticism, but I don't mean it that way. I mean I'm sorry. For the leap."

Howard puts on a conciliatory smile and affects an it's-nothing shrug. Though he feels a tweak of guilt about the deception, he is mostly grateful to slip the noose. The stuff he cut from his story on the fly would have made it clear that he was indeed—in the Saigon bar, for a brief time, behind his eyes—open to the possibility of something quite a bit more with the nameless young woman.

Open to it, he reasons, but he never acted upon it. And the deception of his wife in this present moment was strictly by omission. He has rendered the rest of the story as it happened.

About which Amanda now says, "You're starting to sound like a real writer."

At this he sparks with self-defining pleasure. Also with justification for his story-editing. The cuts served the story's aesthetic clarity. They also served Amanda's emotional well-being. Howard is well aware that only three nights ago he himself had an eruption of jealousy over a figure in his wife's past who had nothing to do with him.

It seems to be going around. But he has the impression that

Amanda is managing her case of it.

And so, for his writer-wife's writing imprimatur, which he knows was probably not an easy thing for her to give to her academic husband, he simply says, with warmth, "Thank you."

March **25**, 2020

Past midnight Amanda arises, sleepless, from her bed. Yesterday's tight little, thin little, eye-averting little coffee-troped story that arrived in a cup vanished with Howard's story. Letting go and rebooting seemed about to vanish, as well. Though he turned her around at the end, for much of Howard's Vietnam tale Amanda was working up to writing about an alternate lover from her own life. Even after acknowledging Howard as a writer, that seeming inspiration lingered with her, elaborated within her, right up until this moment. A tale to tell to try to cauterize this … what? A thing that can break out at the mere appearance of a hairdresser in a New Haven bar or a bargirl working a hotel in

Saigon. Events from times when Amanda had already vanished from his life. Neither of which flirtations apparently went anywhere. Still the outbreak. She mulls on, furiously: *Cauterize what? Some sort of retroactive jealousy. Mine. That was Howard's affliction. My equivalent was long ago. But good Lord. It's still with me. A story of sixty French girls singing. Now here I am, all these years later, getting jealous over possible long-past lovers of Professor Howard Blevins, age seventy-two, for Christ's sake. And it sure as hell has to be about more than that. It's how these tales themselves are going, with the mortally grave state of the world outside our window. We're caught up in a plague-enforced retrospective of our lives. All of it coming at age seventy-two. So maybe it's not quite jealousy. It's just the full assessment of what our lives amounted to. All of it. Not just with each other but with all our others. This is what's weltering away in me now.*

"All right," Amanda says. Softly. And again: "All right."

She finds that she is already standing beside the dining table, where she needs to begin again for tonight.

And even before her mind can shape the next pair of obvious writerly questions—*Ah, but begin where? To write what exactly?*—she knows the answers.

ଔ

So for the next eighteen hours—save for a few of them spent in sleep before sunrise, though even then with her very dreams fumbling at it—Amanda works and reworks her new story.

Now she is sitting across from Howard, prepared by the protocol to read to her husband, but in fact utterly unmindful of him. She wrote this strictly for herself. The literary fiction writer in her maintains both a deep working intimacy with her unconscious and a godly, crafting distance from it. But these visits to that unconscious place have been in search of—have

demanded—literal truth. Not invention. Impervious to a separate, craft-driven agenda. So in this first normalized rereading
of her story, Amanda is prepared to be surprised, even shocked,
at what has come out of her. What she has recalled. And given
what inspired this story, she also finds herself on the cusp of
being terrified.

⭒⭒⭒

THE SEVENTH TALE
Amanda

I danced in my dreams as a child. My feet upon my
father's shoes. My feet were bare. The dancing was also
a waking thing, a real thing. But there, in the recurring
dream of it, I did not feel like a child. Papa was an adult
and so, I felt, was I. Or at least adulthood meant nothing. And in the dream, *his* feet were also bare, where
his Oxfords usually were. His naked feet and mine were
pressed together, but all the rest of him was still veiled in
gray flannel, his coat and his vest and his pants, the legs
of them descending to a cuffless fluttering against me as
we danced. He was teaching me to waltz. And he was
mine. Mine alone. Which was the feeling that endured
when I awoke.

For those first couple of years, I did not know what
my mother knew when he vanished for days at a time.

He was a banker.

Whenever he returned and he and I were alone
together and I would ask where he'd been, he would say,
"Away on business, little muffin." And later it was, "Away

on business, little darling." And later, "Away on business, my sweet young lady. Come, let's dance."

His answers to my question, how they evolved, convinced me in those crucial who-am-I years that I was growing in his estimation of me.

Meanwhile, the shouts were muffled. Of my father and my mother. Always behind closed doors. Not that I wished to hear. I knew that much instinctively. To put my hands over my ears. To retreat to the farthest room in the house. Or into the yard.

After the shouting he would go.

Once in a while, instead, Mama and I would go.

Till we three were home together and it began again.

But Papa and I would also begin again.

In those years when I fit upon his shoes—before I truly knew what the bodies of women and the bodies of men meant to each other, wanted from each other, did to each other—before my own body made a bloody proclamation of its readiness for those same things—I did have a foreshadowing. It came to me as a strange contentment with the fury between Mama and Papa behind that closed door. Even as I wished not to hear the words themselves.

What I felt but did not fully understand: He was mine, he was not hers. He had to be mine. Only mine.

Yet I loved my mother. Genuinely. And I had a child's pity for her. And for him.

"Where's Papa?" I would ask the next morning while she whisked breakfast eggs for the two of us and it was clear he had not returned.

"He is away on business," she would say.

That was as livable a lie for her as it was for me.

Until it wasn't.

On what morning? Some morning when I'd outgrown his shoes but not yet him. We still would dance. But not as often. And with my feet on the floor.

The changes were about to begin in my body. For that new sort of body, he had other bodies than mine. Never mine. To his credit.

But in mine there was the matter of an imprint. His. Even as the fully actionable bodies in his life were creating this other drama unbeknownst to me, having nothing to do with me. Until it was knownst. And had a great deal to do with me.

Mama and I finally, inevitably, spoke about what was happening.

I was sitting at the kitchen table.

The skillet was heating.

She was adding a spillover tablespoon of half-and-half to our four eggs in the mixing bowl, the dairy being the secret she kept for a mother's divine scrambled eggs. And then the pinches of salt and pepper. Her fingertips knew just how much, knew it by the nuance of granules and grinds. She resumed her whisking.

And she asked, "Your chest still tender?"

"Tender," I said. "Yes."

"A little?"

"No. More than a little today."

She nodded and whisked.

Then she stopped whisking.

Ready, I assumed, to turn to her skillet.

But she stayed with me. "Soon," she said.

I knew what she meant. Not the scrambled eggs. My body. Its change.

I shrugged.

She put the bowl on the table and the whisk inside.

Mama hesitated.

The protocol of breakfast called for her to make a smoothly transitioned turn to the warmed skillet for buttering and for me to ask an accompanying question, Where's Papa? The former allowed for the latter to be asked without having to involve each other's eyes.

But on this morning she was not buttering. She was looking at me.

I knew some things already about Papa's time away. Pieced-together things. Still not fully coherent things. Things that had been fumbling around in my head for some time. And now I knew to ask, "Is Papa gone?"

She knew I meant *gone forever*, and I knew she knew when she answered, "Yes, he is."

And I thunderously understood it all.

Though in silence. Unmoving.

So Mama took up the butter and its knife from the tabletop and she turned to the skillet and she did what she knew to do.

Though she hunched forward to do it.

There were sixty of them, or so their first record album proclaimed the following year: *60 French Girls Can't Be Wrong!* But soon after Papa vanished, they were on the radio with a single in the Top 100. Singing incomprehensibly in their own language, but all those girls in one blended multitudinous voice, and they were my age, the age I'd recently been and the age I was and the age I was soon to be and the disc jockeys would unctuously announce these girls called *Les Djinns* and their hit single and how adorable they must be and I heard their voices

sing clearly—and comprehensibly, through their tone—
sing *dancingly* and *barefootedly*, and then when their full
album came out I'd turned fourteen and things were even
clearer—about what my father was doing elsewhere—
now and through all our years together—about how others were giving him the things I could not—and they sang
kissingly and *wooingly* and *knowingly*, these French girls
who couldn't be wrong, sang of their own past with him,
sang *invasively, transgressively,* sang *imprintedly* about
what must be mine alone in order for it to be the beautiful thing it had to be. And so the virus had taken hold in
me like herpes, the virus of this *jalousie bizarre*, alive in
my nerve roots and ganglia, never to go fully away, and
I could see these *others*—sixty of them, one at a time—
singing for my father, dancing with my father, knowing my
father. Knowing him in ways I could not.

ॐ

Amanda has finished with her story. She folds her laptop
screen. Shut. But she does not lift her eyes. She can see them all
now, arrayed on risers, the French girls in their Fifties tea dress-
es. But their mouths are shut. They have sung themselves out.
After her musing, after her trancing and writing, after her reading aloud what came from all that, she feels something let go in
her. After every story she's ever written well, after every novel
she's finished and polished and published, there has been this
same feeling. Something that was complex and oppressive and
true that had been shaping itself unawares within her for a long
time has now crowned and clambered and wailed its way out of
her and bounded across the room and flung open the door and
dashed out into the world.

So she can begin to go on.

She lifts her face.

She is surprised to see another face there.

But of course.

It is her husband.

He says, "Are they still singing to you, this time about me, the French girls?"

It's a good question.

She doesn't answer it instantly.

Howard says, "I didn't even buy them a drink."

She is still slow to be with him. In her, the sixty of them have only just now vanished from the risers. The stage is empty. She is taking that situation in.

Howard says, "I told them, 'Cassez-vous de là.' Which is a somewhat moderated *fuck off*, is my understanding. But I can be even ruder with them if it would make you feel better."

Amanda is not impervious to Howard's effort to be supportive and mood-brightening, even more or less charmingly so in a Howardian sort of way. But it's too soon. It's not the mood she's ready for. Though she realizes she will appreciate it later. Maybe in the morning.

Still. "Thank you for understanding," she says. "It's actually okay now. They have left the building."

"For good?"

"I think so. Yes."

She thinks a bit more.

And she says, "The truth of writing it has set me free."

March 26, 2020

Her back is to him as she sleeps.

He has written. But distractedly, he has felt. Perhaps not distracted. Perhaps defeated by his intransigent self.

Thus he slips carefully out of his bed and rises and takes the single step to stand over her.

She has not stirred.

This intention that has come over him is to wake her. But gently. He lifts his hand. He bends to her.

His hand hovers.

She is sleeping deeply.

He withdraws his hand, stands upright again.

Still, he remains.

He understood her tale this past evening. He of all people would.

But that understanding is rendering itself now in terms natural to the Howard who puts her off. Thematic terms. The terms of the scholar. Terms of the mind.

He thinks: *Sex is the lie that there is no distance between us.*

And about this idea Howard experiences the paradox that he sometimes induces in himself: He *senses* its truth. He *feels* its truth. Which is, in this moment, a slow, dark-gaping dilation in the center of his chest. And the insistent shallowness of his next breath. And his next.

He needed more of that at his computer this evening.

He returns to his own bed, lies down, covers himself up to the chin, shuts his eyes.

His chest has closed its phantom breach.

Seeking sleep, he tries to visualize the Vietnamese mother of a half century ago sitting in naked bulb light in a back alley of Saigon. And he sees her child in her lap. That girl—Howard has only in the last few hours become convinced the child was a girl—the image of that little girl has drawn him to the tale he will later finish for this evening. He hopes with more success. She drew him, but the story is not about her. It is about another girl child.

His mind fills.

It is barely past midnight.

He begins to write. With a rush.

Three hours later he has a tight 746 words. Sufficient unto themselves, he feels.

And he sleeps.

☙

When Howard wakes the next morning, he finds Amanda at the open closet door slipping a black shift over her head in place of her Paris quarantine jeans and Amherst T-shirt.

When her head appears, she sees him. "You awake?" she says.

"I am."

"We're nearly out of food. I need to go out."

"It's permitted?"

"I googled the rules. It's strict. But for a few things it's okay. Groceries qualify."

"My story's finished," he says. "Thank God for the sanctioned excuse. I'm going out with you."

"There's a permission form. We don't have a printer but you can do it by hand. Mine felt like writing an absentee excuse for Dani in grade school."

So after coffee and the last of the croissants and after taking up the two resident burlap grocery bags, Amanda and Howard step out of their building and onto the Rue Botzaris.

They know this city well, viscerally, the densely peopled and dynamically aural Paris. And so they are both thumped motionless by unmitigated street silence below and concert-hall bird song above.

From the plane trees all along the opposite side of the street and from the park's lushness beyond, the redwings and the blackbirds, the wood pigeons and the European starlings, a morning host of house sparrows, and a few high-circling crows all sing in an oddly cohesive mélange of sound.

Howard and Amanda stand still and take it in.

"Let's go slow," she says.

"Absolutely," he says.

They cross the street, entering the roiling chirrup of sparrows, and then turn south to stroll beneath the canopy of trees, the park scrolling by behind a high iron fence.

Almost at once they pass two concrete public ping-pong tables in the road verge and both chuckle that Paris of all places should evoke an American teenager's basement.

A short distance onward is a bench and Amanda abruptly sits at one end. Howard goes a step beyond and stops. He turns to her.

"Fuck the gendarmes," she says. "Let's linger for a few minutes at least."

"Sois jeune et bats-toi," Howard says. Be young and struggle. A crowd chant from their Sorbonne days.

She closes her eyes and tosses her head with a reminiscent smile.

Howard has remembered the phrase and those days objectively, noting a passage of life they shared. Her gesture makes him aware of this state of his mind. He wonders what specific moment she is seeing inwardly now.

But her recollection of linked arms in a Latin Quarter student crowd passes quickly and she lowers her face again to him. She nods at the empty end of the bench. "Dix jours ça suffit," she says. Ten days is enough.

Howard puffs a chuckle. They have been in their Paris lockup for just about that long. She has rewritten another chant from 1968, "Dix ans ça suffit," ten years is enough, meaning de Gaulle's rule.

Howard sits, an arm's length away, still mindful of the gendarmes, his burlap bag visible on his lap.

They bask silently in the open air.

While basking, Howard casually considers how different the open air feels down here at street level—with walking room all about him—than the same open air feels in the confines of their balcony eight floors up.

Amanda casually considers their French, Howard's and hers. He has a better memory for it. Her vocabulary has slipped away over the years. Her little joke was from the chanted drumming of that phrase into her and recalling a simple alternate word.

French voices stir them both from their respite.

Each has heard these voices before.

A low, intense dialog has approached and now passes before them.

Howard and Amanda both think they can place the speakers.

They watch the backs of the couple heading north, a middle-aged couple, she wearing a flowered dress with a cardigan and a pale blue cloche, he wearing jeans and a leather jacket. Each carries a tote bag of groceries.

Opposite Howard and Amanda's building the couple turns to cross the street. But they pause at the curb. They face off. Their voices are faint from here but clearly heated.

Amanda cannot make out the words. She whispers to Howard, with confidence, "I know that couple from before. I heard them from our apartment."

"I've heard them too," he says. "Going on like that."

The woman says something sharply and the man strides off the curb, the woman following, a pace behind.

"Could you hear what they were saying?" Amanda asks.

"The husband said, 'Bête comme tes pieds.'"

It does not occur to her to question Howard's assumption that the man and woman are married.

The couple approach the door to the apartment building.

"Feet?" Amanda asks. A word she thought she recognized from Howard's French.

"You're as stupid as your feet," he translates.

As the man reaches the entrance, the woman has fallen farther behind him, slowing as if purposely challenging him to wait for her. He opens the door and steps through, not looking back, making his own point.

She catches the closing door in time and enters.

The two of them vanish.

Howard says, "Just before they crossed, she called him a 'sack of shit.'"

"Ah," Amanda says, thinking of the husband's insult. "But I don't understand the feet."

"I think it's a common insult. The point on the body farthest from the brain."

"That *sac à merde*," Amanda says, disturbed at the husband and his insult.

Enough so that she rises from the bench.

She steps away, heading south.

Howard rises and follows. "Do you know where we're going?" he asks.

"Not yet," she says, but she lifts her phone and waves it at him over her shoulder. "Google Maps."

She soon is guiding them onward with a clear destination.

At the end of Rue Botzaris they enter the Avenue Simon Bolivar, the plane trees taking the turn with them. They say little, still taking in the quiet of Paris as a kind of meditation, passing storefront tailor and pharmacy, locksmith and plumber, hair salons and cafés. Only the pharmacy is open. A small market is also open. Howard slows a step as they near the end of its one-meter-spaced entry line. But Amanda moves on with: "We can walk farther. There's another up ahead. Let's push our one allowed kilometer to the limit."

And so they arrive at the Priya Market.

In discovering the place Amanda recognized the name as

Indian but saw from Maps' street view that it was a general grocery store and even showed, from a sign in the window, that it carried newspapers.

The Priya's waiting line is shorter. Howard and Amanda maintain their distance from the others and each other and are soon inside.

Near the door is the rack of papers, which Amanda locates at once. "They have the international *New York Times*," she says, and by their next step an Indian girl no more than eight or nine years old stops them.

"Masks please," she says. In English, having heard them speak.

They pause.

From a fistful she offers a pale blue surgical mask.

They each take one and put it on.

"Sorry," Howard says to her. "It's our first time outside since the *confinement*."

"I understand," she says. Both he and Amanda have heard a solemnity in her voice from her first words. She has pigtails and wears jeans and an oversize long-sleeved T-shirt that falls past her waist.

On her left arm is a black armband.

"We have masks for sale," she says.

"They're on our list," Amanda says.

"The white ones are better," she says. Urgency in her voice now. As if this is personal to her.

Amanda reaches to her, squeezes her left shoulder lightly, briefly.

As they pass her, Howard says, "The white ones. Thank you."

"It will say on them *KN95*," she says.

And so they shop, and when their baskets are full, Amanda slips back to the rack at the door to get a copy of the *Times*. But

Howard sees her linger there a few moments, and she returns to him without it.

"No paper?" he asks.

"The Moron-in-Chief says it's just the flu and the precautions will cause even more deaths. So he intends to totally reopen the country on Easter Day. For now, I don't really want to know what else is happening back there."

"I agree," he says.

They go to the cashier counter.

The Indian man sitting at the register looks up from the countertop.

He is wearing a white mask.

He is wearing a black armband on his left arm.

His pompadour has no gray, his only wrinkles being the frown furrows between his brows, and Amanda senses him exert his will to unfrown these for his customers, the relative slow motion of the act speaking of his struggle.

He nods.

They nod.

She begins to unload her bag and he begins to ring up each item. After her bag is empty, Howard puts his on the countertop.

The first item from Howard's bag is the box of masks.

The man watches it descend before him.

As he picks it up to scan it, Amanda says, "Is she your daughter?"

He looks her in the eyes.

She asked this by impulse. She knows she has made a couple of leaps of connection from the box to the question, but he understands before she can explain.

"She is," the man says.

"She's wonderful," Amanda says.

"She is," he says.

He scans the box of masks.

"I'm sorry for your loss," Amanda says.

He puts the box down and stares at it for a long moment.

She fears she's gone too far.

But he lifts his face to her and says, "Her mother. My wife. Lost to this terrible thing that is only beginning."

Then he takes a carton of eggs from Howard's hand, and that is that.

Howard and Amanda step outside.

The chorale of birds has largely dispersed, though the lingering voices are still quite clear in the silence of the street.

They begin to walk back along the Avenue Simon Bolivar, each carrying a full bag of groceries, Amanda with hers clasped against her chest by both arms.

But unawares they walk more closely to each other, letting their shoulders touch now and then.

They both feel small.

Their struggle with each other in this city feels small.

☞

So they enter their apartment and they unpack their grocery bags and they cook and they eat and they drink some wine. And having already on this day whiffed mortality together and turned away from all that's fit to print, they find that they are sealed once again in that other world of private rooms and the bodies and passions within. They face each other before the French doors, and they have recovered the issues and the import of Amanda's last tale told.

Howard asks, "Did they sing in your dreams?"

"Sing?"

"Last night. In your dreams."

121

"The French girls?"

"Yes."

"No," she says.

"Good," he says.

"Listen to you." She smiles very slightly.

He does not quite understand what she means, but as if he does, he offers: "That's perhaps a bad habit I'm already aware of."

He means the habit of listening to himself as he speaks and in such a way that it affects what he says. *Conceptifies it*, he thinks, heckling himself with a made-up thinker-word. *Loftifies it.*

All of this while he is opening his laptop. Having just listened to himself on the subject of listening to himself, thus digging in deeper with that bad habit, parody notwithstanding.

And also while Amanda has been saying, "I know that habit. This isn't the one. On the contrary."

His laptop is open.

Her last declaration sinks in.

He looks at her.

She still has the smile on her face.

He says, "You're still smiling that hemi-semi-demi quaver of a smile. What is it exactly I needed to hear if I listened to me?"

"That you imagined French girls singing in my dreams," she says. "And just now. Your recognition of a telling smile."

He hears approval in her voice.

He shrugs. To downplay her approval. To dismiss any need of her approval. Even to let the scholar within him off the hook, the scholar he has so long nurtured and even admired. And yet he also shrugs to disavow the rough spots of the tale he is about to read.

And he reads.

❧

THE EIGHTH TALE
Howard

She was weary from the ordeal of birth. So was our daughter, who was swaddled in her mother's arms. When we returned home from the hospital, Amanda settled at once into the overstuffed chair with its back to the living room window.

I sat on the facing couch.

The two figures were utterly still. The mother looked down at the child. The child upon the mother's lap stared upward, but at no one.

I thought of the Pietà. Michelangelo's.

Howard abruptly stops reading. "Jesus," he says. He looks up from his laptop. "That was Jesus the expletive, not Jesus the statue."

"I figured as much," she says.

"It's a simple fix," he says. "To cut a bit."

"You listened to yourself," Amanda says.

"I did. Give me a few moments."

He looks back to his written words.

He edits. Cuts a chunk. Tweaks a little around the edges. And he resumes reading, backing up a few sentences.

I sat on the facing couch.

The two figures were utterly still. The mother looked down at the child. The child upon the mother's lap stared upward, but at no one.

He stops again. It is not to think. It is to feel. But it is to feel about thinking. His Paris paradox.

After a few moments, Amanda asks, "What?"

He doesn't know quite yet.

Neither does he hear her voice having already begun to go hard.

He looks at the words.

He lifts his hands, fiddles his fingers over the keyboard.

When he bent to them to fix them he knew the passage to cut. He should step back out of St. Peter's Basilica. Give old Michelangelo and his block of Carrara marble a rest from exegesis. But why? And though he feels a vague other stirring, he concludes: *That passage was true. Of my thoughts at the time and, hell, true in and of the thoughts themselves. This cut is just about a cleaner narrative focus of the story. Intentional aesthetics. But to cut it is to portray the experience as other than it fully was. I promised her to be true.*

"Howard?"

"What?"

"May I make a suggestion?"

"Please."

"Just read the story as you wrote it."

"All right," Howard says. "Let me do some restoration."

Amanda executes a swoop of the hand that says *Carry on,* and Howard returns to his text.

He fully restores the Pietà cut.

But he knows there's one more thing.

He says, "Please let me edit one other passage before I read. I promise you: It will be in simultaneous pursuit of both literal truth and aesthetic quality."

"Sounds righteous," she says, her voice loosening a bit. "Go ahead."

"I need your help."

"Well well."

"I'm serious."

She squares her shoulders to him. "All right," she says.

"It's help from what you called your 'primary métier.' The body's senses. I shirked and shammed with abstraction and generality. But still I *wanted* to do it right. It's a moment with Daniella. More than four decades ago."

He pauses. Even now, again, he tries to remember her directly with his body.

"What is it?" Amanda asks, gently.

"Sorry. I haven't said."

"No."

"Her smell. Dani's smell. The smell of a newborn. At least I knew to try. But I failed. How do I write it down?"

Amanda smiles at him. "Welcome to the club."

"I remember only the one time. There are still some things in me about the newness, and I imagined some others truly enough. But not the smell. Though I know it was striking."

And Amanda says, "Even a mother, who has lived closely with that smell for a few weeks, has trouble. Even a writer mother. But somewhere in the inextricable complexity of it is maybe vanilla, maybe straight-from-the-oven biscuits, and it gets even more vague from there. Condensed milky maybe. Or flowery or soapy. The specifics of those can go anywhere, and no mother can really say, except that this wee thing in her arms smells great. So have at it, well-intentioned neo-sensualist. You mix any of that stuff together in any way you want and no one can dispute you."

"Thank you. I need some time," he says.

"You're welcome. I need some wine," she says.

She rises from her chair.

His hands rise to his keyboard.

☙

An hour later, Howard calls Amanda and she sits down before him once again, the better off for two glasses of Café du Midi Merlot, 2019.

He has rewritten the flashpoint passage. Feeling, indeed, that the impulse somehow came primarily from his hands. Perhaps even from his senses, from opening himself fully, at last, to the good scent of his newborn child.

And the Pietà remains, comfortably, as previously written.

"Start from the beginning," she says.

And he does.

> She was weary from the ordeal of birth. So was our daughter who was swaddled in her mother's arms. When we returned home from the hospital, Amanda had settled at once into the overstuffed chair with its back to the living room window.
>
> I sat on the facing couch.
>
> The two figures were utterly still. The mother looked down at the child. The child stared upward, but at no one.
>
> I thought of the Pietà. Michelangelo's. Christ in his mother's arms. I thought of the work of a maverick scholar by the name of Hilloowala who deconstructed the marble's portrayal of Christ's body—the "forensic pathology" of it—especially given Michelangelo's rigorously acquired knowledge of human anatomy. Hilloowala concluded that from the artist's life experience and from his psychological insight and from his temperament, his aesthetics prevailed. Michelangelo subtly defied the powerful tradition of his era's portrayal of the Pietà. He created

a loving Madonna and Child rather than a grieving Virgin Mary and dead Christ.

I rose from where I was sitting.

Amanda lifted her face to me.

"May I?" I asked. I nodded at Daniella.

"Approach?"

"Yes."

"Of course," she said.

I crept these few steps, wishing not to disturb the child, wishing for her to continue seeing whatever it was she now could see.

I arrived before her.

I looked into her eyes.

And all I could imagine in her was incomprehension. A pressing question for which she did not yet have words. *Who am I?*

An inevitable—a universal—newborn child of a question. But one that will not go away. One that has matured and endured inside me, for instance, even to overripe adulthood: *Who the hell am I?*

Daniella's eyes were vast and horizon-blue.

She was swaddled about her body but her head was free, resting against her mother's upper arm. From my view above—distant still and having tried to enter through her eyes—her head was redolent of incipient thought, of stunned sensibility.

And I understood at once why the Vietnamese believed the head was the most sacred part of the body. And their belief elaborated itself onward, insisting that one's head should never be touched by someone's hand. Especially the top. Especially the top of the head of a child.

My knowledge of this had once filled me with self-satisfied awareness in a back alley of Saigon, where a mother held a child upon her lap, and the two might as well have been a traditional Pietà, the child might as well have been dead, it was so thin, it was so still, and I might have accepted the look of its mother as an invitation and approached. From where I stood, my hand wished to touch the child, to reassure it, to comfort it. Wished to touch the child gently upon the head. But I kept my distance. I understood the culture. I did not even draw near.

And looking at my own child, my *Daniella*, speaking her name to myself in her presence for the first time, I understood how strongly I disagreed with the Vietnamese in that one matter of their belief. The matter of touch.

I drew closer to my daughter.

I extended my hand.

Gently. Gently there, I laid the palm of my hand on the crown of her head.

For many Vietnamese this taboo had become a matter of secular courtesy. But for many others this was still the place from which the soul would pass from the body in death.

She was warm here.

Softly befurred.

And it struck me: This tender place on my child, fully comprehended by the palm of my hand, was a small door from which a vast incorporeal thing would someday pass. But her death was unimaginable to me. Instead, I had a sudden stunning sense that this door had only lately swung closed behind her. Daniella's very soul had entered into her here, beneath my hand.

I bent to her now.

To kiss her head.

And the scent of her entered me.

Stunning in my nose and on into my nasal cavities and down the airways large and small of my windpipe and lungs and through into my very blood, this declaration of Daniella's physical arrival to the human condition. And yes. One can thrash about to describe this scent with the things of kitchen and garden and field and sun. But the effort of that, the compromise of it, reduces the ravishment. The ravishment of her arrival. The ravishment of the very *idea* of her.

So I kissed her.

And I understood: My thought of her soul was not theological. It was not analytical. It was not even metaphorical. It was something from the empty places of my skull.

❧

An artful dodge, Amanda thinks briefly of the passage about Dani's scent. Leading, of course, at last to the declaration of an idea. But she is still stuck on the part she urged Howard to restore, and she returns to it at once. The passage about the Pietà. Upon which she does her own analysis. She thinks, *One way for analytical discourse to legitimately exist in a passage of literature is by point of view and dramatic irony. By the sensual presence of a personalized narrative voice and its emotional subtext. The focus shifts from the ideas of the analysis to the emotion of the speaker, that he should be moved by his feelings to express these particular abstractions in this particular narrative moment. And with that shift, literature arrives. In the case of Howard's aspirant literary passage—and this is a conclusion I am unable to avoid—the emotions revealed are of a deeply flawed personality. Aloofness, obliviousness, estrangement are feelings too, after all. The speaker of his story—this* true *story—him—upon the very first arrival of his wife and newborn child into their home—instantly, drastically he distances himself from both of them by an extended, tangential scholarly retrospection. Either Howard recalled and recorded his deeply disturbing emotions of the time or he has written his own deeply disturbing retrospective emotions from the present. And if the latter, with the same emotional distance, he is smart enough to analytically recognize these implications of the passage and wish to quickly back away from them. To prevent me from seeing him—yet again—as he is. So he researches the smell of his child and hides behind a rendering of what he has learned. And throws in some knowledge of a foreign culture to boot.*

All of this passes through her as Howard sits before her with—what's that?—a fucking tear in his eye. Expecting it to be proof of something no doubt.

And for his part yes, Howard feels the tear well up and he feels it to be appropriate somehow, and he goes at once to work understanding it in his characteristic way, even as it comes to fullness in his eye, and he understands those felt empty places of his skull to signify the locus of his fault, and the tear brims over and tracks coolly down his cheek and it has a meaning for him, a theme, and the theme is a word, a word he forms in his head now: *redemption*. Perhaps even two words: *redemption* and *justification*. This, he concludes, is what this uncharacteristic event—the shedding of this tear—is about. He does not wipe it away. Nor does he reconcile—does not even recognize—the incompatibility of those two abstract words, as he deeply wishes them both to be true.

Meanwhile, Amanda recognizes her own recent real-life first-person internal-narrative voice, alive in the subtextual way she most cares about. But what the hell? At this of all times it masked itself by her ready use of the very rhetoric she so often scorns. The rhetoric of ideas. She offers herself a fleeting mea culpa. And she reruns it all: *My first moments at home with Dani in my arms, and her father—my husband—this man I met and we fucked and we parted and I happened upon him again and we fucked we married we fucked to this eventuality—her father sat before us both, having just brought us home from the birthing and I understand him, finally, one way or another, and what now he has most resonantly fucked—as in fucked over—is that precious, transcendently emotional moment.*

And through all of this Howard and Amanda sit silently before each other in their cross-back side chairs in front of the French windows of their Airbnb apartment in Paris, Howard's computer closed in his lap, his hands resting there, Amanda's arms lying along her thighs, unmoving.

They stare directly at each other, but in this moment they do not actually see.

What she has done in her head—even if somewhat improved—is not enough. She needs narrative of her truest sort, of the moment, of the body. She needs clarity.

She lifts her elbows and tucks them against her sides. She draws her two hands together before her face, tents them, pauses very briefly, then touches the tips of her forefingers to her lips. To collect herself. To modulate her voice into seeming dispassion.

She parts her hands and lowers them to her lap. She unobtrusively clenches them into fists. A tell-tale sign which she has no choice but to risk.

She does not expect him to notice.

He does not.

"I see your tear," she says with lull-the-jerk gentleness.

He lifts his hand to his face in reflex, wipes the track of it away. "Sorry," he says.

"No," she says. Oh so sympathetic. "*Display* it."

She regrets the verb. It reveals her felt, sarcastic subtext. She needs to keep that hidden.

But again Howard seems not to notice. He nods just a little, as if tastefully accepting a compliment.

She lets him have that moment uninterrupted. Then: "May I ask a question?"

"Of course," he says.

"I know you arrived at that …" She hesitates very briefly to consider the best word to achieve her masked intent, even considering *redemptive* before letting it go. And she finds "… *self-reflective* moment."

"Yes," he says.

Self-reflective is clearly just swell for him.

And she says, "But my question is: That very interesting take on the Pietà, was that your presently blossoming scholar-cum-writer self at work or were those indeed your thoughts of that precise moment in 1980?"

"Oh, those were my actual thoughts," Howard says. "But I wished to withdraw them from the story because the blossoming writer in me—and I cannot tell you what sweet satisfaction I have from your sensing that in me—my writer self heard how that might prompt a misleading aesthetic response in a reader. But this isn't fiction. It's truth."

"Of course," Amanda says. Again she considers her strategy, and she stifles her next words: *Or might prompt a close reader to thus interpret the climactic emptiness of your skull to be an irrecoverable wasteland rather than a neglected place restored.*

She forces her hands to unclench.

She knows this could all fall apart quite easily. But the contagion is still abroad. She and Howard are still trapped.

She rises from her chair. Silently. She has a tale to write. That will do. It always has.

She turns and goes.

Howard, for his part—neither having noticed his wife's knuckles gone recently white nor having close-read her recent line of questioning—is more or less content.

March 27, 2020

She is stuck.

She knows that yet again she must restart a story.

Her MacBook screen awaits her. Fully tweaked. Style: Novel. Set for Multiple Pages with a beginning Page Break and her customized *WRITING* toolbar hidden and the Zoom slider at 120 percent to display two empty white pages so as to fill her screen on a black background.

All very familiar.

But she is stuck. Though only lately discovered, the Pietà is also very familiar. Familiar from the get-go in her life with Howard.

Has it always been inevitable, an escalating estrangement between her and her husband? Will it always be?

Surely this is the stuff of the tale that her screen awaits.

She thinks to simply write from the place where her mind presently lingers. Just hours ago she drew Howard out, but to prevent a personal meltdown between them she deliberately didn't confront him over the timing of his covert monograph on a Renaissance statue. A timing that seems to her wildly inappropriate, even for him, given that their child was swaddled between them in their home for the first time, still scented from her birthing.

Amanda can confront him tomorrow, with her own story about all of that. Say the things she didn't say to his face tonight. But the priority of his brain—the priority of his heart—on the day that the birth of his daughter was so dramatically portrayed before him: that was utterly unknown to Amanda until those few hours ago. And its essence foreshadowed their life together in the following years, an essence that has been a muttering motif in the tales they've both told on these past eight nights.

So her impulse shifts. She should go straight to the first marriage breakup itself. The end of the twenty-two-year first act of the novel of their lives. *What happened to end us*, she thinks. *What he did.*

Her hands rise to the keyboard.

There were two separate scenes at that climactic time. The first of them is known only to her. Her hands are ready now to tell that untold tale.

In the second scene she could have revealed it. But she did not. For what seemed to be good reasons.

Those reasons once again check her.

She puts her hands in her lap.

She does not write. But she revisits that second scene in her head. From a little distance.

I sat in our living room. I'd arrived from a conference in Austin in the early afternoon, and Howard was arriving from San Francisco in the early evening. I had time to unpack, which I did in slow, meticulous motion, though with the slamming of a dresser drawer or a curse into the empty air along the way.

Then I sat in one of the two overstuffed chairs in our living room. Mine. His empty beside me. I read a book as I waited. Some book or other. For several hours. A well-written book perhaps but now long forgotten even in its title, for I was barely comprehending it while waiting for Howard to come through the front door.

Then he did.

He saw me sitting.

He saw me take a deep breath and place the book carefully on the table beside my chair.

He put his bags down.

He straightened too.

There was a long silence between us. I was struck by his seeming intuition. There was no reason for him to think this was a homecoming different from any other. Unless, in the emotional physics of a marriage there can be a gradually developing critical mass where a fizzle at the end of the chain reaction is, in fact, the detonation. And for him the end had come.

And I realized that I greatly preferred a fizzle to an explosion, which I could easily detonate with my tale. I just wanted out, at last. Why blow us up now when a thousand circumstantially contentious things from the past were enough to fizzle us to an end.

I billowed in relief.

I composed my voice. Mild but firm. Implacable. "Please sit," I said.

He did not move. He registered my words by not registering them.

And when he'd waited long enough that it was clear it was of his own volition, he went to his chair and sat.

The two chairs were separated only by the table and were angled slightly toward each other. The default sightline was across the room. We needed to consciously turn to look at each other.

This we did.

We did not speak for a time, however.

I imagined even that I could hear his brain grinding away, abstracting the thousand little things.

Was I aware that my present assessment, my choice of approach, my chosen balance—or, rather, imbalance—of mind over emotion, my consciously sought refuge were very much the same as my husband's own inbred preferences? Preferences that were a major issue of disconnection between us?

Of course I was aware.

To recognize and to embrace the irony of that made it my own.

At last then, I said, "Being apart this time …" I hesitated, sorting through neutral ways of saying what was next.

But he spoke first. "Was different?"

That would do. "Was different," I said. "Yes. From other times."

"Yes."

"And yet not different." I let that be for a moment.

He did not answer.

But I was watching him closely, and Howard the detached thinker was clearly the Howard who was sitting beside me at this moment. His eyes stayed fixed on mine by positioning, but I strongly sensed the mind behind them looking away in serious thought.

Which apparently concluded: "A tipping point," he said. "A tipping point can be both different and not different. Usually is, in fact."

Just so.

The tipping point was what we'd come to.

For that, we both understood enough. What I knew to tell was not needed.

That was two decades ago.

But now.

Now she thinks: *We draw near to another tipping point. It demands that I tell what I know.*

She lifts her hands to the keyboard.

But the narrative voice in her head abruptly turns on her and says, *Wake the fuck up. You write that story in the usual way and read it to him tomorrow, and you just give him a chance to answer back the next night with a close read of his own rational and righteous butthole.*

And she abruptly knows what to do.

She rises. She crosses to the closed bedroom door, pauses, lifts her hand to it, and with the knuckle of the forefinger of her right hand raps on it.

Once. She waits only a moment and then, fully expecting to have to wake him, she steps in.

The night table lamp is on.

Her eyes fall first to the bed before her. His. Assiduously laid out there is his sleeping costume, as if he were in it. A long-sleeved T-shirt and open-leg sweatpants, both black and both pocketed for nighttime tissues and scholarly brainstorm note cards.

He stirs in her periphery and she looks to him. Before the closet door, Howard has turned to face her. He is stripped as far as his boxer shorts.

"We need to talk," she says.

He does not reply at once. She knows he's reading her words, assessing the tone of her voice.

She intervenes. "Briefly," she says.

"All right then," he says, and he gathers up his pajamas.

She steps aside as he moves past her and through the bedroom door, heading for the bathroom.

She remains standing at the foot of his bed.

She tries to stay calmly focused on what she must do. Just that.

He comes back, hesitates in the doorway, dressed.

And she finds that she pities him a little. He would not strip off his boxers before her, not to complete his intended dressing ritual, not even to quickly slip on his sweatpants. She thinks: *How long has this modesty been going on?* And then: *That I can't answer the question is itself the answer to an even more pitiable question. About both of us. But this is not the time to consider that.*

Still he stands in the doorway.

"I want to change our rules," she says. "Maybe only this once. But certainly this once. I want to write about *that* night."

She hears herself and realizes he might think this is still about bringing Dani home. She pauses to seek identifying words that can be clear without being inflammatory.

She starts to clarify: "The *first* …"

"Ending?" he says.

"Yes."

"Of us."

"Yes."

"You sure you want to change the rules? They worked beautifully. We embraced them for the lawyers and the divorce court, but let's face it, they worked for us too. Big time."

He pauses, even as she realizes he's thinking of the legal rules. *Irreconcilable differences.* The legal outcome of the homecoming scene she has only a few minutes ago recalled. No one had to charge anything, no one had to admit anything.

She has other rules in mind now, but his intuition seems to have been activated again. Before she can clarify, he continues, "Have you forgotten? For once our compulsive bickering yielded. We said only what was strictly necessary not just to the court but to each other. We made those rules by instinct. They were the *right ones*. We got away from each other cleanly and simply."

"But we never expected to be *here*, remarried and figuring it out again, nineteen years later."

Howard loosens at this logic. He realizes he has no reason to hold anything back from a complete, mutual assessment of their marriage. No matter how problematic. As for the writerly challenge, he feels confident in himself. He shrugs.

"It's time to undo all that," she says. "Right here. Right now. Do we know what we want? Should we just shrug and call it irreconcilable differences once again? Then it's already a done deal."

"Did I shrug?"

"You shrugged."

Howard finally steps from the doorway and into the room. But one step and no more.

Amanda says, "I said it vaguely, and you made a perceptive close read. You're right. It's not about that initial night between the two of us. I'm going to write what *brought about* that night. The inciting incident."

Howard draws a slow, deep breath, straightening at the spine. He thinks: *Just so.* And he says, "Are you sure that's what you want?"

"I'm sure."

He hesitates for a moment. But yes. He will say this much: "I have an inciting incident of my own."

"Oh really? Fine then," she says. "What I'm actually propos-ing is best for us both. I think we need a *new* rule. For *this* tale. A procedural one. As we've agreed, I'm going to write as fully as I can. Full truth. Full disclosure. So of course you'll think you have to tailor your next tale as a response. Especially given our similar topic. But even if you're not writing from some lawyerly subset in your analytical brain—even if unintentionally—your story will inevitably be different if you hear mine first. More argumenta-tive. And less *true*."

Howard humphs.

Before he can protest she rushes on: "I'm sorry if that sounds ad hominem. If you were writing first, I'd get twisted into doing the same thing. It's human nature, obliviously lying to oneself from the pressure for a rebuttal. And then unintentionally lying to the other. So. Great. You've got an inciting incident. Let's *both* of us get to work on stories about that. But at the same time. No deadline. However many days it takes. Whenever we're finished, we'll both read on that same evening. I'll still go first, as it was my turn next, but we'll read back to back with no editing on the fly."

She's done.

As the following silence begins, there is but a minuscule pause in Howard before Amanda jumps in for some special pleading. "That's why we're in Paris, isn't it?" she says. "To figure us out in the best way possible?"

And he says, "Yes, it is."

March 28-30, 2020

For the first time since their first morning in Paris, Howard and Amanda have breakfast at the same time. Not together, simply adjacent to each other. They nod, they sit, they eat, they drink, and then she begins to write in the bedroom and he begins at the table. Having said absolutely nothing through all of it.

Howard expected this silence from his wife. He knows the ways of these rarified creatures he has devoted his life to studying. One of the two central characters in the story she is writing—her putative antagonist—happens to be manifest in flesh and blood beside her. And it's not even fiction. Given what he knows of her process, she has no choice but to act as if he isn't there. He respects that. He also learns from it, thinking, *Beware, my particolored rainforest bird, you take me for an ornithologist, but I'm quietly perched on a limb of the next tree over.*

Concurrently, Amanda thinks, *Okay, Howie. Try to make things complicated by keeping a respectful silence. You're close-reading me like mad, and you're smart. I know that. It's why I've always kept on trying to make things work with you, telling myself that one kind of smart implies the existence of—or at least prepares for—another kind of smart. Smart in the heart. A kind of smart that your innate kind of smart, however, can contrive to simulate when you've analyzed a situation just right. So eat your fucking breakfast and write your version. You won't be able to juke and fake and lie so well without hearing my truth first.*

And the silence between them more or less endures through that day and night and the next day and night with the only words spoken being brief, formal, and commonplace until, on the morning of the third day, Amanda says, "I will be done by noon," and Howard says, "I should be done by late afternoon."

Evening, March 30

Amanda and Howard approach the cross-back side chairs before the balcony doors, each of them carrying their laptop.

They sit.

Silent still.

Amanda opens her MacBook and begins to read.

THE NINTH TALE
Amanda

In the fall of 2000, we each left town on the same day, my husband and I.

We bought new cell phones for the occasion, ditching our Motorola clamshells for tiny new Nokias.

Howard headed to Madison, Wisconsin, and I to Austin, Texas. For him, a conference with fellow modernist scholars, all of whom were in the midst of fending off both post-structuralist and postmodernist scholars widely attacking modernist writers for their numerous cultural and moral shortcomings. Or some such. For me, an appearance at a book festival to do a solo reading and then to sit on a panel of two. My new book was a collection of a dozen short stories titled *The Wives of Wausau*, each in the voice of a different woman who is in love with someone other than her spouse in Wausau, Wisconsin, and is trying to figure out who she is. The other panelist was Billy Jay Jessup, born and reared, bred and busted, in the town of Merkel, the county of Taylor, the state of Texas, and thus he was the prime attraction for the festivalgoers on this Friday afternoon in the state capital of Austin. I was paired with him because we shared a publisher and, in an essential way, a concept. His new book was a collection of a baker's dozen of short stories entitled *All Hat, No Cattle,* each in the voice of a different man who is still living in Merkel or has mistakenly thought he's escaped Merkel and is trying to figure out who he is.

Rather like the author himself, I suspected. He had a hat all right, a black Stetson, which was the first detail of him that I noted as he approached the stage of the auditorium in the state Capitol Building Extension. The spectators were arriving and I was dutifully early, standing behind our table, speaking to a bright rotunda of a lady librarian who was to be our moderator.

He came up the steps and across the stage and there were things about him besides a hat. Girlish-big dark eyes like groupies to his mannish jut-jaw and cleft chin, a complexity like the hat paired with his school-boy blazer and perfectly Windsor-knotted tie.

He now stood before me, perceptibly closer than I was accustomed to with most anyone. His height registered on me in the lift of my face to his, the strain at the back of my neck reminding me that Howard was five-foot-nine. And this guy was put together such that I might expect him—my being a Wausau girl imagining a Merkel boy—to have been shaped by wrestling steers, not syntax.

"Amanda Duval?" he said.

"Billy Jay Jessup?" I said.

"May I bypass *howdy* and get straight to *shake*?" He offered his hand.

"Shake," I said, and I offered mine.

His hand was large like the rest of him. But he took mine and instantly made the crotch of our thumbs fit tightly together. He presented another complexity: The shake was firm enough to be buddy-buddy for another man but just restrained enough to whisper gentleness to a woman.

Not that I intended to let on about any of these impressions.

"We've got two stages of friends where I come from," he said. "If you're in the lesser, you're howdied but not shaken."

"Glad we jumped ahead," I said as we continued to shake.

I flipped my face upward just a bit more—a gesture toward his Stetson—and said, "But I'm thinking you're a man without cattle, Mr. Jessup."

He lifted his own face a little and barked a laugh. After which he reengaged my eyes and finally relinquished my hand. With just a bit of a squeeze, in punctuation.

"Not *all* hat," he said, and he removed it and, without looking, plopped it on his place at our panel table. "And forgive me for not taking it off to shake hands with a lady."

I'd been expecting a pumped Texas accent. His stories were strongly voiced—I'd read some on the plane and liked the way he inhabited his characters—and there was the pitch and strength in his spoken words that I'd expected from listening to the Texan men in his work. But I could not hear an actual accent in him.

So we sat beside each other, and to a crowd of a hundred or so Austinites Billy Jay Jessup and I talked about Merkel and Wausau, men and women, the short story form and the novel form, and we nodded at each other now and then in the transitions, as the questions alternated between us, but our librarian behind her lectern made no effort to get us talking with each other, and then the hour was over and the applause was over and the auditorium was rapidly emptying as our librarian thanked us and dashed away.

Billy Jay Jessup and I had lingered at the table and now found ourselves standing before each other with another handshake in the offing.

I abruptly found myself wanting to banter with this man. "So," I said, "Looks like it's happy trails time."

He smiled at me. "That how they say it up your way, is it?"

"To be honest, rarely."

"So it was for my sake."

"When in Rome."

With this, both of Billy Jay Jessup's hands lifted before him, plummeted downward, and with dramatic casualness his thumbs inserted themselves into his black jeans, on either side of his silver belt buckle. Which portrayed a cowboy on a bucking bull.

And starting now to stretch and undulate his words in the accent I'd been expecting, he said, "Don't rightly know that place. Are you by any chance talking about Roma down in Starr County?"

"I reckon I am," I said, though voicing it as they would up Wisconsin way.

Then in full-blown, honey-oozing, Texas self-parody, Billy Jay Jessup said, "Well, little lady, since we been eyein' each other for more'n an hour now, seems to me we need to meet up after this whole book shindig is over. We can grab a Lone Star and hear some music down on Sixth Street."

Though said in the spirit of it, this was clearly something more than banter.

Not that that sentence passed through my mind in an analytical way.

Far from it.

Indeed, one of those hands of his immediately emerged from its thumbing and touched me gently on the shoulder, and Billy Jay Jessup said, with no Texas put-on at all in his voice, "Seriously."

And I flashed on twenty-two years of my husband, the years fast-framing in me in a way that felt very specific, very imagistic but wasn't quite; that was, instead, a felt summary of specifics, an instant grasp of countless individual images: My husband in moments when he was full of pretense and pose, when he was full of put-on that he wasn't even aware of about something in some other part of his life but that also inevitably implied or ignored or exacerbated something important inside me, and I waited for a moderating word from him, a calming gesture, but one of my husband's hands did not touch me gently on the shoulder. It did not. Instead, one of his hands circled behind him, tucked itself inside the back of his pants, extended its thumb and stuck it up his own asshole. Metaphorically speaking.

Meanwhile, Billy Jay Jessup was still arranging things. "Why don't I pick you up at your hotel round about 7:30. You at the Omni too?"

I was still flashing back and trying not to let myself flash forward, so I couldn't speak for a moment, though I was aware a question had been asked.

"Is that okay with you?" he said.

I found that I'd actually heard the previous question. And the proposal.

"Yes," I said. "The Omni. And yes on the picking up."

"Sorry it's not dinner," he said. "I'm already booked with a reviewer from the Fort Worth paper. I'll talk you up to him if he doesn't know you. He's a good man."

And I heard myself say, to my surprise, "You don't need to put a professional spin on all this."

Two simultaneous, very slight movements—a dip of the head and a lift of the eyebrows—and a subsequent beat of silence from Billy Jay, with his eyes fixed on mine, gave me an inordinate fillip of pleasure.

His eyes stayed with me as his hand reached for his Stetson, which still sat on the table. Reached and flailed just a little bit before grasping it and putting it on his head.

"Well, thank you kindly, ma'am," he said, the accent oozing back in. But moderately, suggesting no exercise of his will to either enhance it or suppress it. He was being suddenly natural with me.

And then Billy Jay Jessup was walking me along Austin's Sixth Street on an early November night, with its Texas balminess working over my Greater-Chicago mid-autumn flesh. The street was crowded. Did we walk close from the get-go? Yes we did. Not afraid for our arms to bump, to touch. Did I slip my hand onto the crook of his arm? I did not. I did not even think to. Did he slip an arm around my waist? Yes. But only temporarily, to keep us together as we tacked slowly through the crowd along the blocks of two-story Victorian masonry storefronts.

The bars called themselves out in neon, with doors open to the drinking and to the music, the country and the jazz and the funk commingling. The Black Cat Lounge and the Blind Pig Pub, Emo's and Plush and Lucy's Retired Surfers Bar. And there were tattoo parlors and street sellers of flowers or of glass doper pipes and there were the nook-and-cranny solo musicians with tin cans or upturned hats. And along the way a flatbed trailer with a mechanical bull to ride for *a buck a buck.*

Billy Jay kept our destination to himself until we arrived at last before the Flamingo Cantina, where a focused flamboyance of bargoers was filing in. He was known here, I realized: We passed the scrutiny of a ticket-taking doorkeeper—perhaps the model for one of his book's escapees from Merkel—and the man simply exchanged a knowing nod with the writer. We needed no tickets. Though there was headliner music tonight.

Inside, the cantina was clogged in the deep but storefront-narrow space, the focus of the crowd at the moment being the bar running down the righthand wall.

"Lone Stars first," Billy said, and he put his arm around me once more and negotiated our way through to a barman and our beers and then, with bottles in hand, he took us deeper in until we were absorbed into the cohesive music crowd.

We all faced a compact, lit stage.

Billy Jay bent to me, put his mouth near my ear, his breath warm upon me, and he said, "Reggae. Great reggae tonight. The Flamingo is a stop for the big names and tonight it's Burning Spear. More radiant than Bob Marley."

Radiant he turned out to be, this man who called himself Burning Spear. The stage was soon tightly packed in the background with his horn section and a trinity of guitarists before them and downstage-right the man himself, lushly gray-bearded, off-beating on a pair of congas before taking up a wireless mike to sing his sweet-voiced solos.

I stole glances at Billy Jay through the concert. Bullrider though he was perhaps bred to be, he was bouncing to the rhythms of a Rastafarian soundtrack to Heaven. Seeming a little radiant himself.

After the concert, we jostled past the bar. Billy Jay bent close again and I presented my ear to him. He said through the noise, "Plum sorry, Amanda Duval, making us choose between music and drink. Let's set that right."

I turned my face to his in order to answer.

He was very close.

I tapped my ear.

He gave me his, and I brought my mouth close to him. "But not Sixth Street," I said. "Somewhere quiet, yes? Let's keep the radiant sounds in our heads."

He looked back to me. He smiled. "You understand." He had obviously shouted this, though the crowd noise muted him such that it sounded like a loving whisper.

We both turned toward the door.

Billy Jay put his arm around me once again, once again having the neutering excuse of working our way through a crowd. But this time the grasp of it was an unmistakable hug.

Which he maintained until we were outside and along the sidewalk a ways and into a bit of a subdued stretch between bars and crowds.

Then he stopped us, and he loosened his arm and let me go.

I said, "Wrestled and released?"

Where we stood, without street light or neon, made it hard to see his expression. But I inferred incomprehension from the tilt of his head. I almost explained: *Steer wrestling. I've seen a TV clip. You grab, you embrace, then you let it go, all calm and you're done with it.*

But I didn't.

He still just couldn't seem to make it work in his brain.

So I said, "What's next?"

He revived. "Quiet is what you hanker for?"

"Yes."

"The hotel then?"

"Fine," I said.

He let the comfy Texan voice return: "Excellent plan, little lady. Lone Star is good. But Tito's Handmade is better."

I cocked my head at him.

"Handmade, homemade," he said. "Texas vodka."

We began to walk back the way we came.

As we turned off Sixth and the street sounds faded, Billy Jay Jessup began to hum reggae.

I finally slipped my hand onto his arm, and he placed his other hand on mine. I said to myself: *This is simply a warm, huggy, peck-on-the-cheek gesture. For both of us. Just a couple of literary friends, admirers of each other's work, fellow travelers on a ship named Random House.*

Commensurate with that thought and not to give any fellow book people at the hotel a misimpression, as we approached the Omni I began to let go of his arm and he gave my hand a final pat in obvious agreement.

And soon we were sitting at a table in the lounge in the lobby, with its twenty-story glass-and-granite atrium fully open above us, its kinesthetic lift lingering in my chest.

"So how do you take your vodka?" Billy Jay asked.

I hesitated a moment. I'd had a nice glass of wine in mind for most of the walk from Sixth Street.

He picked up on my hesitation. He leaned toward me across the table. "It's vodka time," he said. Unaccented.

Both plaintive and insistent. His eyes were still girlishly, darkly beautiful.

And by now we had a waiter standing over us.

"Martini." And because of those eyes of his, I said this to Billy Jay and not the waiter.

He nodded. "That's okay for right out of the box," he said. "Though don't forget we're playing catch up. The evening's a little ripe. So how do you take it?"

I looked up at the waiter. "Wet, please."

"I'll have what the little lady is having," Billy Jay said. "But dry. Both with Tito's."

The waiter departed.

And Billy Jay started talking about Tito's Handmade Texas vodka.

"Sweet corn's the secret," he said. "Stead of rye or wheat, or potatoes for God's sake. Sweet nibble on the tongue. And lookee here. Texas was way behind making anything but hooch. Hell, the Tito fellas were the first legal distillery in Texas since Prohibition. And that was just three years ago. But they made up for lost time. Believe you me."

I started to fade when he got off on the Tito boys using a pot-still rather than a column-still, their way being much more labor intensive.

Then our martinis came and we clinked and he drank and I sipped. He downed his martini as if he needed to quench a thirst. I still had plenty of sipping to do as he ordered more Tito's, this time three shots neat in a tumbler.

When it arrived he saw me eye the glass.

"Just a reminder," he said. "I know where I want to git to and I got the horse to ride. But no spurs now, just mosey."

The tumbler did seem to slow him down. After nearly slugging the martini, he was taking the straight vodka in a glass almost meditatively, talking about the demands of book touring. But halfway through the tumbler, meditation turned to vituperation about a specific reviewer, and having made his point Billy Jay grabbed the tumbler and gave it an angry look.

He put it to his lips.

Two-fisted. Literally.

I felt an ill-defined urge.

"Can you excuse me for a minute?" I said.

He looked at me. Lowered the tumbler a bit.

"Just a couple of minutes," I said.

I stepped out of the lounge, and well out of earshot, into the lobby. I dialed Howard's Nokia on mine.

The impulse in me remained ill-defined. But I wanted to remind myself of Howard.

The phone was ringing.

Part of me was ready for him simply to be himself. Thoughtful Howard.

The phone was ringing.

Though that readiness was also ill-defined.

The phone was ringing and then it wasn't and there was a fumbling and a muttered something or other and then Howard finally spoke a recognizable "Hello?"

"It's me," I said.

More fumbling.

I thought I lost him, but then he was back. "Amanda," he said.

"Yes."

"Where are you again?"

"Austin, Texas."

"No wonder that didn't stick in my head."

"No wonder," I said.

"I'm in Madison, Wisconsin," he said.

"I know."

A brief pause now.

I didn't blame him. This call was not typical between us when we were on the road.

"How's the book festival?" he said.

"Fine."

Another pause.

"I'm in my hotel room," he said. "About to go out to dinner with some colleagues. Running late."

And now my ill-defined urge to talk with him turned abruptly into indefinable and then quickly into meaningless.

"I'm sorry." I felt the need to give him some excuse for my call. "I just wanted to see how your war council was going," I said, drawing improvisational inspiration from my sense of irony. That I should care. "Over those wrongheaded postmodernists. Are you ready to kick their asses?"

"What?" he said.

I didn't know if he was asking me to repeat what I'd just said because he couldn't hear it clearly or if he was asking why the hell was I calling about something he knew I didn't give a goddamn about.

I had no answer either way.

"I won't keep you," I said.

"When we get back," he said and he paused. As if that was a full statement.

This was madness.

"Sorry," I said again. "I'll see you Sunday night."

"Yes," he said. And I heard him begin fumbling with the phone again. Hanging up, I suspected. He and I were still learning the keys on our new phones.

Still awaiting a verifying good-bye and keenly aware of how bizarre I had just sounded, I was rendered motionless just long enough for his voice to recede a bit but say quite clearly "It was her."

And for a woman's voice to say, "You didn't have to answer."

This I surmised: He'd needed to push the *Navi* key, which controlled the power, but had pushed the nearby *Scroll* key instead.

"I didn't want her to call again," Howard said.

The woman muttered something indistinct, and then she said, "So we've got a working thesis. Come unhook my bra and let's do some research."

I found my own Navi key quickly, expertly, having mastered that fucking skill in my first hour with the phone. Unlike my rarefied academic husband. Though I felt I should be glad he had not.

So that was Howard.

A much larger ill-definition had suddenly defined itself quite clearly.

I just needed to decide what to do about it.

I started to move across the lobby floor, heading back to the lounge.

I'd had temptations before this.

Of course I had.

I am a creature of my body.

Any artist is, at their core.

But I always wrote one story at a time. Wrote one book at a time. My creativity demanded that. *Fuck me,*

I thought. *I can* read *only one book at a time.* That body I was a creature of had an all-in sensibility. So it had been with my marriage.

I'd flirted a little, in recent years. But those were just opening paragraphs. Not even partial drafts. Quickly abandoned.

I neared the lounge. I could see the table inside where the Texas cowboy with a knack for narrative voice sat. He was drinking deep of his vodka. The tumbler tipped high. His head reared back.

He was using his spurs.

I stopped just outside the lounge and watched.

The glass came down, empty. Immediately he straightened, turned, motioned to the waiter, who came and heard him and followed his head nod to the empty tumbler, receiving an order. Another one of these.

So this was Billy Jay Jessup.

But goddamn it.

I entered the lounge.

I arrived.

He looked up and his head wobbled faintly in surprise to find me standing over him.

"Howdy," he said.

I stayed standing.

Sizing him up one more time.

His dark eyes were still beautiful.

He rolled his shoulders. "I mean shake," he said, offering his hand.

I ignored it.

"How far gone are you?" I asked.

"Only a pleasant buzz," he said. His voice sounded steady. "I'm good at this."

And I said, "Well, cowboy, here's the deal. Do you want to get drunk or do you want to get laid?"

He chose laid.

❧❧

Amanda has read rigorously from the screen, not once glancing up to her audience, and she now follows the lid of her computer in its closing.

When she lifts her face, Howard has been waiting.

His eyes are fixed on her, at first seeming so in a way familiar to her, as an outward manifestation of his intensely engaged rational mind. But she quickly realizes it's not so *simply-Howard* as that. There's something else here. This fixedness has a faint gawk to it, a look betokening a search for but an utter failure to find an expected rational understanding.

Or so it seems to Amanda.

Howard's look, in fact, has something of surprise in it, certainly, but the gawk is more from irony than anything else. He does understand.

He thinks: *It is best just to read my tale.*

And so he begins.

❧❧

THE TENTH TALE
Howard

She was at the opposite end of the table, to my left. A Dorothy Richardson scholar, named Dorothy herself in 1958 by her suburban Philadelphia housewife mother who was trying to figure out if she was anything other than that and who therefore was moved, avid reader that she was, to track down the twelve volumes of Richardson's *Pilgrimage* through interlibrary loan in the only available British edition and was in the midst of reading number eight, *The Trap,* when the eventual Dr. Dorothy Hayes of UC Berkeley emerged from her womb. Thus explained by Dr. Hayes herself in just such a run of modernist-tinged rhetoric. I turned my face and leaned a little forward to look past the profiles of two other scholars to see her.

She had a Nefertitian profile, with a long slide of a nose, and she was waving her cat-eye-glasses from a table-propped arm as she spoke.

This was an event at only the second annual convention of the defensively conceived Modernist Studies Society, and we were all of us featured on this panel in order to defend our discipline, to enlarge our discipline, to justify our discipline, to—in the words of the rubric of the moment—*Recontextualize Modernist Literature.*

All of which we did, aptly enough, in one of a half dozen "Hall of Ideas," on level 4 of the Monona Terrace Convention Center, in Madison, Wisconsin. But I lost sight of her when our event was over, and after shop-talk delays along the way from our panel table at the other end of the room, I finally stepped through the doorway onto the enclosed Grand Terrace.

Ahead was a sweeping view of Lake Monona, its surface a vast, blandly uninflected gray, edged thin-ly all along the far-shore horizon with a dark sort of green that one could only assume indicated trees.

A figure I recognized was standing alone at the

window looking outward. She was easy to identify, even from this new angle, with her tightly bunned caramel brown hair and her cable-knit sweater evocative—willfully, I was certain—of the iconic Yousuf Karsh photo of Hemingway taken the year before she was born. I approached her and after having just gone through an hour of fluently speaking and hearing a cognate-laden separate language—Academian, if you will—I felt the influence of all that in my plan to engage her. *Hello*, I would say, *I read your recent Journal of Modern Literature article, "Islands in the Stream: POV and Time in Dorothy Richardson." You have achieved clarity at last for the true original in the triumvirate.* And in giving her namesake preeminence over Joyce and Woolf in the development of stream of consciousness as a mode of narration, it would be strictly an intellectual flirt with Dr. Dorothy Hayes.

And I arrived beside her at the window.

She turned her face to me and smiled. "Dr. Blevins," she said.

"Dr. Hayes," I said. But then I said, "You're far-sighted."

It was not what I expected to say.

But she heard an abrupt compliment—*perspicacious*—and she replied, "Thank you. Modernism should expand, it is clear. Temporally yes. Spatially yes. But the vertical—that will bring us dangers. Into popular culture? Please. We must not lose our focused essence on *literary text*. We are aestheticians, not sociologists."

Her panel points. Far-sighted. Yes. But not in the language I found myself having unexpectedly, impulsively just spoken with her.

I translated: "I meant your eyes." Which, in response, instantly widened to figure me out. These eyes could, with some evocative accuracy, be identified as lake gray, but that body of water in our periphery besmirched the color. This was, upon her, a color neither bland nor uninflected.

I said, "Your glasses have vanished. As at our panel." And I even lifted my hand and gave it a bit of a spin, recalling her waving of them.

She gave me a nodding, upturned frown. "I do wave them when I talk, don't I."

"You do," I said.

"And you often do this," she said, angling her head slightly to the right and lifting her right hand, extending index and middle fingers and lightly tapping her temple. "While listening to others make their points," she said. "Elbow established on the tabletop, eyes respectfully on the speaker."

"Indeed?" I asked.

"Indeed," she said.

She let me absorb this indeeded observation for a moment.

Then she added, "And if we had been to your right? Are you an ambidextrous temple tapper?"

"I'm not sure," I said. "You're enlightening me."

"Enlightenment is our job, is it not?"

"It is. But you had already discerned your own gesture. *I* am shamefully clueless."

"Ah," she said. "But my gesture is there before me, visible. Yours is out of your sight. You have no other physical sense at a thoughtful distance to perceive and analyze this bodily gesture."

"Finely observed and discerned, Dr. Hayes."

"Thank you, Dr. Blevins."

"I'm flattered that you noticed," I said.

"As so you should be," she said.

I bowed to her, from the waist, slightly, briefly closing my eyes.

When I straightened from the bow and opened my eyes to Dr. Dorothy Hayes, she was smiling, also slightly, and in response she lifted her hand and made the waving motion that, without the eyeglasses in this context, troped onward to become the gesture of a queen acknowledging a crowd.

Which prompted a simultaneous smile.

Our panel had taken place in the last time slot of the morning sessions.

"Had you planned to eat lunch?" I asked.

"I had every intention," she said.

"The Hilton is but a few steps away," I said. "They have a restaurant."

"I'm staying there," she said.

"So am I," I said.

"So I inferred," she said.

An inference that led to a Hilton Hotel restaurant lunch, where we resumed speaking Academian. Subtext and synecdoche over salad, mimesis and metaphor over the main course. And through the afternoon we remained together, attending panels of paper presentations on such things as hypodiegetic narration in James Joyce and feminist historiography in Virginia Woolf, and then onward together, the two of us, for a Hilton Hotel restaurant dinner, during which we were assiduous in our professionalism, and we remained so even during a subsequent extended Hilton Hotel lob-by-bar mostly wine session.

However, as the evening progressed, the academic in Dr. Hayes began to perhaps, shall we say, blur the boundaries between herself and her subjects, arriving eventually at what might even be interpreted as an epiphany. She tilted over our table-for-two and monologued, "Scholarly papers ah papers, papers don't you love them? Exegetic are they not? Peering always into the deeper things. Even when they do not realize what they are seeing. So do not listen with your ears when they are read out. Listen more deeply into the written texts themselves. It is revealed there even in the printed program. Today did you see? *Tropic Transformation in Joyce*. Of course: The adjectival form of *trope* to all of us in our sect. But only to us. And only when spoken aloud from our brain. But even for us is it not also what is revealed on the page? Is it not another thing there? *Tropic*. As in the always warm climes. *Tropic Transformation in Joyce* indeed. Jimmy and Nora at a resort in Bora Bora and him transformed there, no longer so sexually enamored of bum holes and farts and shite but with prime focus at last on the parts that a woman cares most about? And do you not also understand at last *Tropic Nostalgia in Proust*? Marcel bedded down and becorked in Paris but beset with longing for the gay bars of St. Barts? So yes and yes. Yes. There were revelations to be had with our own ears as well, during lunch. Listen again to our profession's words as they spoke their secrets aloud. What did we dwell on as we ate? *Synecdoche*. The part standing for the whole. But hear it spoken and then give it a close read,

Dr. Blevins. Oh my. *Sin-neck-dick-key!* What a subtextual story, yes? The thing potential lovers will do: *sin!* The spot of his first kiss upon her: the *neck!* And then. The part that really is standing for the hole, standing *up* for it: the *dick!* The sexual act resides within the very word itself! And to finish the exegesis, the means that she gives him to enter her hotel room: the *key!*"

She paused, a little bit breathless.

She summed up: "Glorious, what we can do, you and I. Yes?"

She paused again.

And she stressed: "The literary analysis, I'm speaking of."

At this she stopped.

She did continue to press forward over the table, however. She kept her eyes uninterruptedly on mine even as her hand went to the half-slip glasses case that had lain beside her since the bar drink menu. Without her eyes flickering away for even a moment she extracted her reading glasses and put them on to study my face.

I took the odd formality of the gesture as an invitation to read her closely, as well.

Glorious what we can do, she'd said. She and I. *Can.* A capability. A *possibility* that she felt had needed an immediate clarification of what type of gloriousness it was that she'd referred to. We'd just spent a day together that was entirely, rigorously intellectual except for one brief flirty exchange and one recent soliloquy redolent of wine and stream-of-consciousness consciousness. So there was no inevitable presumption, in a context of Joyce and Proust, that a sexual deconstruction of a literary term—even if it had involved a hotel key—was offering her listener a quite personal invitation. Which, therefore, would justify the interpretation of her ostensibly clarifying declaration as ironic. Which meant this was indeed an invitation to a sexual encounter.

These thoughts passed quickly through me as we stared at each other over the table. And yes, they were thoughts, which spoke to a further irony. For even while I was consciously reading her, I was also taking in her whisperingly-blue-as-well-as-cloud-gray eyes, revisiting their color as a remembrance of a thing past—muted now, as they were, in the low-light of the bar—but also experiencing them vividly in this present moment as quite stirringly unblinking, with no thoughts of their own at all, her gaze simply leaning warmly against me. Further, I found through all this that her own studious scrutiny of me being framed by her twirlish cat-eye reading glasses somehow suggested a double plot, weaving together a dual narrative of body and brain.

We stared on.

This ongoing suspension between us identified itself to me as the high time when I needed to consider my wife.

And immediately I discovered a double plot of my own. One of its two storylines argued to my mind that this consideration would best be done somewhere other than a bar and should definitely be done alone. The other storyline was stirred and allured in my senses, even more keenly so because the transformation of the woman before me was apparently tropic enough for her in the trope of a warm hotel room, her own similar double plot thus evidently integrating itself into one. Perhaps legitimately so, even if achieved largely through wine and dead, randy, modernist writers.

For the moment, an intermediate action struck me as a workable compromise.

"I think it's time to head upstairs," I said. "Tomorrow's plenary session convenes quite early."

The latter was, strictly speaking, true; the former had to be done this evening no matter what. Asserted together, they effectively delayed any drastic decisions.

In the elevator I stepped at once to the panel of floor buttons and pushed *10*. My floor.

I thought, *Let* her *decide this.*

I stepped back from the panel, not looking at her, making way for her to come push a different button.

But she was not coming forward.

The door closed.

I looked at her.

She was standing next to me, an arm's length away.

She was returning my look. Intently.

Yes, I thought. *Some blue in the gray.*

"Same for me," she said.

"The same?"

"Floor," she said.

"Ah yes," I said.

"The conference block of rooms," she said.

"Will we be able to sleep?" I asked, intending to immediately clarify my jocular intent by expanding on its irony, declaring how all the modernists will rowdily keep us awake through the night, implicitly in our separate rooms. But the joke got caught somewhere inside me. I was not sure if in my mind or simply in my throat. Whichever it was, I was also not sure whether my failure to clarify was from an end-of-the-day weariness or from a not-yet-fully-recognized intention of my own.

"I don't know," she said. "Will we?"

I faced forward and waited for our floor.

That question was a seriously uncertain this-or-that, as well.

The bell dinged.

The door opened.

We stepped out of the elevator and walked along the corridor, saying nothing more at the moment.

My room was coming up. I had no idea where hers was.

So I again let her decide what was next.

I stopped at my door. No *Come in* but no *Good night*. I simply took out my wallet and opened it to retrieve my magstripe room key.

The rustle of her on the hotel carpet ceased.

She had paused nearby.

I found the key and I lifted it before the lock. But I hesitated for a few moments to indulge a fantasy I'd delayed long enough. To speed-read the Abstract of an academic journal article on my marriage. Twenty-two years in the researching.

My wife would have me recognize—have everyone at the modernist conference, indeed have every scholar in every English Department everywhere recognize—that the product of their thinking souls is purely secondary in the world of the objects whose essence they are seeking. Recognize that in art, the moment is paramount, the feelings are paramount, the body is paramount. That language, the medium of literature, should be as irreducible and experiential in its perception and understanding as are color and form or pitch and timbre or gesture and step and leap in the other arts. And if humans are living a dual narrative of mind and body, the thinking part needs be absorbed into an enhancement of the moment, of the senses, of the feelings. In art. In life. In marriage. In a singular encounter, for that matter. In a hotel room. So I will suggest in this paper that by my wife's very own intrinsic aesthetic sensibility I should cease analyzing and simply fuck this other woman.

I had become aware, in the pause for this, that Dorothy Hayes had rustled on along the hall.

I looked now in her direction.

She was standing before her door, two rooms down.

She was looking at me.

As soon as our eyes settled upon each other, she said, "I have a theory about the final 583 words of Molly Bloom's concluding soliloquy in *Ulysses*."

For a long moment her words—granularly academic—seemed to refute the conclusion I had just come to.

She waited patiently, however.

And certainly Joyce and his Molly and her yes yes yes soliloquy were, for a scholarly woman, inherently sexual.

So I managed to reply, "Sounds intriguing."

"I need a collaborator," she said.

"Of what sort?" I asked.

"Of your sort," she said.

"To *collaborate*," I said, trying to inflect the word so that she would know I was not being thickheaded but aware.

"We will need one room or the other," she said.

"Which?"

"Mine would better fit my deep-diving read, since Molly is in her own bed."

"So she is," I said.

I looked at the key in my hand.

Was I ready?

I was indeed beginning to stir in the relevant places, both emotional and physical.

"You may come as you are," Dorothy Hayes said, close-reading me.

So I put the key into my wallet and turned and she was already unlocking her door.

I approached and she was standing inside, holding the door with one high-lifted hand and welcoming me in with a sweep of the other.

At the far end of the room the blinds were open, and the window framed the floodlit State Capitol building and its approaching boulevard.

She led me along.

We reached the bed and at its window-side she paused me with a touch of my arm and stepped away to the night table lamp.

She switched it on, turned back to face me, and she pulled off her cable-knit wool, voluminously turtle-necked, fisherman's sweater and tossed it away to the floor.

Standing before me in a black bra, she said, "Throughout the book Joyce has hidden in text and narrative-action countless references, historical and literary and linguistic. We need to recognize that he makes a final such elliptically subtextual joke with us in the form of a climactic action hidden in the conclusion of *Ulysses*. Leopold Bloom, who lies beside his wife in their bed through the whole soliloquy, actually sexually enters her. He does so at the very moment of and thus prompts—and is thus revealed by—her unconnected, interjected, intrusive exclamation of *ah* in the first of the final 583 words, and from thereon, even as Molly maintains the flow of her own independent stream of consciousness, he fucks away to final climax, both hers and the book's. I have the 583 words precisely memorized, Dr. Blevins. I want you to fuck me now, and I will recite and track the correspondent progress of my own orgasm in comparison to Molly's."

"Have you ever gotten them to match?" I asked.

"Not yet," she said.

I'd prompted this last exchange without conscious forethought, and before I could assess it, from my inner tweed jacket pocket, my cell phone rang.

It was a new phone number. It could be only one person.

Dorothy Hayes knew about my of-the-tribe-of-our-subjects wife. Just as I knew about her never-read-a-word-of-literature boyfriend. All learned quite matter-of-factly and comradely along the way.

The phone rang again.

"The author?" she asked.

I nodded.

"I am discreet," she said, and she placed her forefinger upon her lips.

Still apparently in a no-forethought frame of mind, I turned my back to the black-bra-bedecked Dorothy Hayes and stepped to the window with its radiant-in-the-dark Wisconsin State Capitol.

The phone began to ring once more and I knew this was wise, my preferring to lie by omission now rather than lie outright later.

I fumbled at the phone and finally I said, "Hello?"

"It's me," Amanda said.

"Hello, Amanda," I said, speaking her name to make sure Dorothy knew for sure to keep quiet.

For a moment I turned inward, as the details regarding my wife at this moment had grown a bit blurry. Nothing in my brain clarified the situation. "So where are you again?" I asked.

"I'm in Austin," she said.

"Right," I said. "Texas. I'm in Wisconsin. Madison."

"I know," she said.

This was a mistake, answering the phone.

But it was imperative that I sound natural.

"How are things at the festival?" I asked.

"Good," she said.

There was a silence.

If she had to call me, I assumed she had a conversational agenda. But she was fucking silent.

"I'm in my hotel room," I said, thinking, *Okay. Not just a lie of omission. But if I have to fill the silence, I need to create an exit strategy from this conversation, whatever that requires.*

And I said, "I'm about to go to dinner. With some colleagues. I'm already a little late."

My mind instantly began to rerun this further lie.

Checking its plausibility, memorizing it for going forward. But the whole Wisconsin situation—from conference panel to bedside bra—limited my ability to successfully hear one thing and think something else in parallel.

So I knew Amanda had just apologized, and there was something about—what?—a war?—and postmodernists and kicking asses.

I wrenched myself back to her.

Okay, war maybe, apparently with postmodernists. True enough, but all I could manage was "What?" As if I hadn't heard her clearly.

"I won't keep you," my wife said.

And for a moment I thought I had *really* missed something. As if this was about our marriage, the not keeping me. Was she telling me she was leaving me? Or letting me go? Did she somehow know what was going on in this hotel room?

None of that was likely.

I could only stall.

I fumbled in my head for words. "We can talk when we get back," I said.

She apologized again, a simple "Sorry." And she said, "I'll see you Sunday."

"Yes," I said.

I took that for a sufficient goodbye between us.

I wanted nothing but to get the fuck off this call. I was already turning away from the window as I found the call disconnect button with my thumb and pushed it.

Dorothy was standing where I left her.

Still in her bra.

"It was her," I said. Dumbly. We'd already established that.

She smiled, but her brow simultaneously wrinkled in concern as she observed my present befuddlement. "You didn't have to answer," she said.

"I didn't want her to try again," I said.

She shrugged. "That makes sense," she said. And then: "So we've got a working thesis. Come unhook my bra and let's do some research."

She turned her back to me.

But I found the stirring in me had stopped: *I try to take a step to her and do what she asks and unclasp her bra and turn her around and say to her yes I will yes, and I tell myself this act will be a pure singularity, it will be as private as a never-read book so it is okay to do this, but these are alien words coming from vainly firing brain cells when whatever is to be done here must be from no forethought yet I find myself full of thought, fore and otherwise, which means there are to be no hands now no breasts no lips no following body parts no Dorothy Hayes reciting no Molly Bloom, no Dorothy and Molly made one with me tonight, and forethought carries me abruptly out the door and into the hallway hurrying along to my room where there will be plenty of afterthoughts but for now for this time for this woman on this night, no I said no I won't no*

Howard and Amanda sit staring at each other for a time. As if blankly.

Finally: "Was that the truth?" Amanda asks.

"Yes," he says. "And you?"

"What? That I wrote I did it, but in fact I didn't?"

"I withdraw the question," he says.

They each think a variation on: *Here demonstrated are the advantages and disadvantages of an irreconcilable-differences divorce.* And they each think how irrelevant that thought is at the moment.

After one more extended stare, Amanda says, "If I hadn't called you, would you have fucked her?"

"Good question," he says.

"So?"

Howard takes a deep breath. "We've been fully honest with each other tonight."

"So it seems," she says.

He nods.

He pauses for a long moment.

In the midst, it occurs to him to explain: *Since your apt question is speculative, my only hesitation is in order for me to speculate honestly.*

He hesitates a moment more.

And then, "Yes," he says. "I believe I would have."

"Thank you," Amanda says.

"Thanks?"

"For the honesty. You could have claimed the moral high ground."

They go blank again for a moment.

Then Amanda says, "I didn't want to sleep with him."

"So why do it?"

"You should be asking a different question."

"What question is that?"

"Why did I call you when I did."

It's a good question, he realizes. "All right," he says. "When you called, what did you want from me that would've kept you out of the cowboy's bed?"

"An emotion."

"Which one?"

"Almost any one."

Howard has no answer for that.

ↀ

The two of them have quietly risen and separated and prepared for bed in silence.

They lie adjacent in the dark.

But they both realize the same thing. Which she speaks: "We can't leave it at that."

"No. We have to write onward."

"From there," she says. "From our shared moment of ignorance."

He agrees with a slow intake of a breath and its slow release.

Which Amanda understands. And more. She says, "But first we need to get out of this place again. At least for an hour. They give us an hour each day, I think."

"Yes," Howard says.

"First thing tomorrow," she says.

"We will. Yes."

March 31, 2020

The next morning, while still within the confines of their Paris Airbnb, Howard and Amanda break their silence only for practical matters. They both must find words to write when they return to this apartment. So for now they simply say what's necessary to negotiate their access to the shower. And to collaborate on making the coffee and the eggs. And to sit down to the creation of their handwritten *Attestation de déplacement dérogatoire*, their permissions to go into the street.

This prompts Amanda to review the regulations on the internet.

Before her laptop screen, she says, "We qualify under 'individual exercise.' I may have overlooked a similar rule last time because groceries are groceries and we both eat in the same household. But here,

they stress that we have to exercise one at a time. Though as long as we keep the one-meter social distance from each other, that should be all right."

"I hope mere walking qualifies as exercise in Paris," Howard says.

Amanda sighs. She jogs, he doesn't. She says, "Just wear your Skechers and your hoodie and I'll dress down, and whenever the cops draw near let's at least pump our arms."

"Agreed."

It occurs to neither of them to question how it is that they reflexively feel the need to stay near each other for this.

Once outside, though, after they step to the curb and both nod to the park side of the street and cross to it, Amanda says, "Can you accept *brisk* walking? The park's locked down anyway. If we creep, we think. We need to prepare to write."

"You set the pace," he says.

And she does. She turns right and strides off east on Rue Botzaris. Howard hustles up till he's two paces behind and then he matches her gait.

Neither of them glances at the passing head-high wrought-iron fence nor at their fateful park beyond, not even as the iron fence briefly gives way to a concrete balustrade for a long view. They look ahead instead, Howard at Amanda's bun of hair and Amanda at the quarter-mile stretch of fence and walkway leading to the intersection where the park turns sharply to the northwest. And they concentrate on stepping and breathing and swinging their arms, both ardently wishing to set aside for a little while the inevitable: their facing the ironies that leaped from last night's stories and the aftermath that awaits in the tales they will have to tell next. And the present deadness each feels in the center of the chest.

Soon they reach the end of Rue Botzaris at an intersection. Ahead Botzaris angles off under another name while an intersecting street leads around the east side of the park. They stop.

They have an arm's length between them but Amanda discreetly sidesteps a bit farther away from him. "Jog in place for the traffic," she says. "Right away."

Howard complies.

Shortly thereafter the Police Nationale Renault that Amanda spotted slips past them. The driver turns his face to them but simply nods as he goes by.

She says, "Want to stick with circling the park?"

"Do you?"

"I was wrong," she says. "Hot pursuit won't get us to where we need to be next."

"Which is our ten years apart," he says.

She taps her chest. "We can't really skip it."

"I know a place," he says. "There's a turning just ahead. With a run of strictly pedestrian side streets. We can slow down in a nook of Paris that will keep us focused."

"All right," she says.

Amanda follows Howard now, and a hundred yards along he turns them into Rue de Mouzaïa. She keeps her distance behind him as they start along a two-lane residential street with a canopy of plane trees. It will continue for a mere third of a mile and giving off it are narrow lanes reserved to pedestrians by a bollard at each entry. On the right, the lanes go uphill, on the left downhill.

As they pass one and then another and another—on the right they are spaced every hundred feet—Amanda looks up the hill each time. The passageways are lined with terraced two-storied row houses in pastel plaster or in brick.

"What are these?" Amanda says from behind him. "These little streets."

"They were created over the homes of a century of quarry workers who mined gypsum until the middle of the nineteenth century. This was all part of the vast space where the last Napoleon created our park."

"I had no idea such a place existed in Paris," she says.

"It's still working people. Retired people. Off the tourist grid."

Howard has not stopped for this exchange, nor looked over his shoulder.

But he thinks to say to her *Pick a lane.*

And she thinks to say to him *You're right about the nook. Thank you.*

But the only spoken word between them follows Amanda's thought. She simply says, "Here."

He stops and looks and she is entering the lane they have just now passed.

He follows.

But he keeps his distance. He senses her seeking her writing place.

And Amanda is thinking, *There are things that my husband and I must write now for each other and those things will have their way with us and we will do something at last or fail to. The plague is passing all around us but I don't feel it here. This is why I wanted to come out in the midst of it. To find a place to make a declaration. Fuck the ironies. Fuck the ceaseless—the inevitably ceaseless—demand to choose between alone and not-alone. Fuck it all except for these cobbles beneath my feet and these passing plaster walls and their iron fences thick with climbing ivy and with wisteria and rosebushes and lilacs fraught with greenery while waiting for their blooms.*

And as these things are happening in Amanda, Howard's thinking resonates back, as it did two weeks ago on their balcony, back to the park that would begin their marriage, back before the park itself existed. *That park didn't just hang men and slaughter horses. It also sent generations of quarrymen with lanterns and pickaxes digging into the depths of its adjoining hills for gypsum to make into the finest plasters to build the finest structures all around the world, gypsum plaster that even built the East Coast of a newly birthed nation. Which included America's White House itself, its very walls and ceilings coming from the earth now beneath our feet. To this day, part of this quarter is called "les Carrières d'Amérique," the Quarries of America.*

Up ahead, Amanda abruptly stops. She draws close to the iron fence on the small fronting courtyard of the nearest row house and looks upward.

And as Howard stops too, he just as abruptly hears himself. *Ha. I know how all that history ended. Paris gypsum built a house for John Adams and a century and a half later for a haberdasher from Lamar, Missouri, who had the place gutted and rebuilt. And who could blame him? The ceilings were ready to collapse on him in his presidential bed. Sure everything changes. Things fall apart. But it's easier to think about that on this little outing the way I always have. Easier and safer. Tomorrow I have to get at what our man Hemingway called the "true gen." To write what's next as truly as I can. And my reflex way doesn't work.*

Amanda has not moved. Howard takes a step closer to get an angle to follow her ongoing upward gaze. She is looking at an unshuttered open window on the second floor. She is fixed on its dark emptiness.

He will wait quietly for her now.

A few moments ago, when Amanda stopped before this house, a woman was in that window. She was there only briefly, staring down to a table in the courtyard. A cat was crouching there beneath it. The cat is still there but the woman has drawn back, vanished.

The woman reminds Amanda of Howard and his man Hemingway, and she feels inspired to tweak both their noses by appropriating the setup of one of Hem's stories and filling it with her own words. She hears them in her head:

The American wife stood at the second floor window looking out. In the courtyard below, beneath the wrought iron patio table, a gray and white cat had compacted itself into utter stillness.

She had not seen this cat before.

She and her husband had rented this small house in the Mouzaïa of Paris two weeks ago.

"There's a cat," she said.

Her husband was behind her, at the small desk across the room. He had not been typing at his laptop for some minutes. He has heard her but makes no comment.

Though she'd partially addressed him, she did not notice his silence. She watched the cat, waiting for even a slight bit of movement.

There was none.

Now, more fully to her husband but looking still at the animal, she said, "I'm going down to get him."

Though his hands had risen to the keyboard, her husband paused. "To get him?" he asked.

"The cat under the table. I want him."

"Why do you want him?"

"His thereness," she said. "It will come with him."

This her husband did not hear. He had resumed typing.

Now Amanda turns to her husband. He is standing a ways off, perfectly still.

She says, "Let's head back."

"Yes," he says.

"You lead," she says.

And so Howard and Amanda walk at a pace just brisk enough to pass for septuagenarian exercise and at a two-stride interval so as not to draw the attention of the Paris police.

They pass beneath the plane trees of Rue de Mouzaïa and then beyond, through the intersection, and onto Rue Botzaris. They stay close to the park's iron fence. The opposite side of the street is now a quarter-mile unbroken array of eight-story apartment buildings leading toward their own.

Amanda watches Howard's back up ahead, trying to focus on the man she must soon write for, considers that these shoulders of his are broad, wonders when she last made note of that, tries to now.

Howard finds himself faintly regretful that he did not ask her once again to lead the way. He is unsettled by taking this walk as if alone, seeing only the street ahead, preferring to watch the bun of her hair.

They are nearing their building now. But they have reached the brief stretch where the iron fence yields to the concrete balustrade, only waist high and looking far out into the park. They both glance to that view and they stop.

In the distance is the Temple de la Sybille on its Corinthian columns, rising free from lake and trees and paths, its garlanded cupola backdropped alone against the midmorning sky.

The place where they began.

Without looking to each other, Amanda and Howard simultaneously move toward the balustrade. And in doing so, unaware as well of the angle of their paths, they converge there and stand beside each other, shoulders nearly touching.

Not that they flash once again to the moment of their first meeting. They find themselves aware of the temporal distance of that place before them, as if it is the final image in the sort of dream from which they wake without an achy back or knee or neck but only with a vague wistfulness. But they each have a faint shudder of dread at the writing they must now do, the feelings that await them in the stories to come.

They each become conscious of the other's proximity, near but not touching. Still, they do not look.

And then the voice of a French gendarme breaks in.

They start and turn and before them is the Covid-masked face of a young man in black jacket and side cap.

"Bonjour," he says.

"Bonjour," both Amanda and Howard answer, though not quite in sync.

The gendarme nods. "Papers please," he says in English.

They dig in their pockets and produce their handwritten permissions.

The young man takes them, reads them both. He looks first at Howard and then at Amanda and he says, "Monsieur Blevins, Mademoiselle Duval, you must keep distance between you."

Amanda and Howard answer at once, together, "But we are married."

ᘓ

Back in their apartment, encouraged by the smiling voice of a Paris gendarme to keep no social distance between them for the rest of the day, Amanda and Howard have one more cup of coffee together, sitting at the dining table.

They are quiet.

They both have a similar wonderment at how a mere hour outside these rooms could benumb them as it did. For the roiling is beginning again in both of them, needing to be given voice.

Each has a similar thought: *For God's sake look where we ended up last night.*

The clink of her cup on the tabletop pricks Howard.

The clearing of his throat grates at Amanda.

Howard says, "With this somewhat shortened day of work ahead and both our tales seriously refocused, are you comfortable going tomorrow?"

"Not really."

"Silence tomorrow seems intolerable to me."

"I agree," Amanda says.

"The rotation could start anew."

"I take it you can be ready?"

"I can. If you can accept two flash tales."

"Your beloved Mr. Cobb's forte," she says.

He hears this as a covert dig at his scholar self.

But he does not respond.

182

April 1, 2020

Howard sits at the tabletop prior to the evening reading, waiting for Amanda to emerge from her writing session in the bedroom. He is nursing his way through a cup of coffee, as he's gotten minimal sleep in order to write what he now sees as his two-part tale. A tale he feels to be a sufficient representation of the decade of their divorced years.

As the caffeine sharpens his focus, he finds himself replaying a bit of the aftermath two evenings ago. And he thinks, *I asked the wrong question. Not "What did you want from me to keep you out of his bed?" It should have been, "If I'd simply not been available to answer the phone that night, would you still have fucked the cowboy?"*

Howard wishes he had phrased it that way. But it's easy for him to think this after the fact. A bit of proof: Without a pause even to consider it, he rejects the possibility of asking it this evening. Or anytime, for that matter. Is he aware this is because it would be painful for him to hear the answer?

Yes.

He doesn't need to hear it. Her answer would have been *Yes.* She still would have.

His rational, conscious mind understands that now.

Too bad. It leaves him thinking this: *There was no way I could have learned on the phone call that she was planning to fuck the cowboy. She called requiring a voluntary emotion from me. For what conceivable purpose? To stop her. It was all that could have. Well how about: "Please don't fuck someone; the very thought of it causes me an acute pain." That might have worked. But that emotion could not have risen up in me without my being able to imagine things playing out the way they did. Which I couldn't without it having happened. So I now end up with: The only way I could have prevented her from fucking the cowboy that night was for her to fuck the cowboy.*

And though this is, to Howard's analytical self, an intriguing irony, it is an excellent example of why this thinking self of his knows to assiduously avert its eyes from difficult feelings in the first place.

Like knowing to keep your distance in the memory of a self-destructive mother.

For another example.

Meanwhile, behind that closed bedroom door, Amanda sits on the side of her bed, her ritually bare feet on the floor now, her MacBook closed.

She does not know how to feel in anticipation of Howard's small stories tonight.

She has herself already written to a stopping point.

Setting the full record straight.

She stares at her bare toes. A husband's blank-brained stumble down a hotel hallway. A cowboy heard through the door of a hotel bathroom imitating the Dixie Chicks in a falsetto.

To hell with it, she thinks.

When she emerges from the bedroom there is nothing she can imagine at the moment to say to her husband, who is sitting in the reading chair with nothing he can think to say to his wife except what is on the screen before him.

☙❧

THE ELEVENTH TALE
Howard

After my wife and I, *irreconcilable* as we were, hid behind Illinois law and said nothing to the court or to each other except that it was done, truly done, it was dead as a doornail, our marriage of twenty-two years; after we commenced living "separately and apart," which is to say I had an alley-view apartment on Library Place, with a six-minute walk from University Hall; after the long-and-slowly-amassed avalanche of all that had finally crashed into silence at the bottom of our marital slope, Winter Recess at both Northwestern University and The University of California, Berkeley began.

So as soon as my relocated computer had been plugged in, I flew to one Dr. Dorothy Hayes, modernist scholar, with whom I had conferred by email regarding our still unfinished collaborative research. She had booked a cottage in Trevone, Cornwall, England, to feel near to and to finish an article on her beloved Dorothy Richardson.

With sea birds crying on a mild Cornish late-fall afternoon, she met me at the door of the cottage, wearing her Hemingway sweater. Her eyes were more blue than I remembered, and we actually kissed for what was the first time ever. We simultaneously remarked on that immediately afterwards.

Now came a flurry of suitcase and outerwear and cottage orientation, accompanied by a brief biographical note from my Dorothy Richardson scholar about her namesake writer's poverty and obscurity in Cornwall.

And then, finally, Dr. Hayes and I stood beside her bed, having arrived there instinctively and without any overt reference.

I said, "Now in the matter of Molly Bloom's soliloquy ..."

And she cried, "May the spirit of Joyce preserve us! But not benighted Joyce scholarship! I was drunk, Dr. Blevins. I was a fool, Dr. Blevins. Caught in an unseemly rut. Let us simply engage in sexual intercourse, you and I, with no thesis and no discussion and no footnotes."

Which we did.

And while we still lay nakedly entwined, I quietly begged her pardon: "I must, however, offer *one* footnote."

"If you must, Dr. Blevins," she said.

I gently untangled from her and guided her onto her back. I rose up just enough to make my way down the length of her. I took up one of her legs, flexed it at the knee.

And I kissed her on the arch of her foot, touching her there with the tip of my tongue.

Uncharacteristically for both of us, we offered no further annotation.

But when I returned to our reclining embrace, she did ask, "Is that a signature gesture?"

"I have done that only once before," I said.

Howard pauses in his reading, keeping his eyes on the screen. To signify the end of the first part of his two-part tale. And yes, to let the epiphany of the first flash have its impact.

Which it does. So before he can begin the second tale, Amanda says, as if matter-of-factly, "Is that it? Your tale for the evening?"

He lifts his face to her. "Just the first of two parts. I told you they would be flash."

"I wondered," she says, maintaining her even tone. "That sounded less like a fully-realized piece of flash fiction and more like a fuck-you note."

Howard waits a moment to muster a reply. None is occurring.

Amanda asks, still calmly, "We agreed these tales we write are to be true. Was this one?"

"Yes."

"Every detail?"

"You mean the kiss on the arch of her foot."

"As you might expect."

In the locked-eye moments of silence that follow, Howard knows well his wife's writing process, drawing details from forgotten things moldered into the humus of her imagination. And he knows his own mind. And her suspicion.

He says, "I have an on-call memory. You're far more likely to commit literary lies than me."

"I know the difference," she says.

"So do I," he says.

With measured dispassion Amanda says, "Just curious then. If that was an on-call gesture for the benefit of your modernist scholar, why didn't you ever do it a second time to me?"

With a flash of passion, Howard says, "Why are we here now, going through all this?"

Both questions having thumped to a rhetorical end in their asking.

As if the first was a manifest indictment.

As if the second was the answer to the first.

In the silence that follows she answers her own question, to herself: *No doubt that kiss was a typically thought-out gesture for a first time fuck.* And she answers his question with a comparably rhetorical shrug: *Who the hell cares?*

Both Amanda and Howard are vaguely aware they are mostly posing with the rhetoric because they are still trying to come to terms with last night.

He returns to his screen.

But he remains silent for a moment, his pause not a focusing transition but simply discomfort. Given the active friction between him and Amanda, he fully expects her to hear the second flash of his story not as a *fuck-you* note to her but as a *fuck-me* note to himself.

So be it, he thinks. *I shouldn't care.*

But he does need to work up a bit of courage now. To revisit this other dissolution. Though it vanished, it once did have its appeal.

So he waits, and then he reads.

For three years they would meet, Howard and Dorothy, by the bay in San Francisco or the lake in Chicago, after one or the other flew the two thousand miles. And often, following just-reunited-sex and a subsequent quiet interlude of a few minutes, the traveler would produce their seat-pocket copy of the inflight magazine and in graduate-seminar instructional intonations would deconstruct a blandly chirpy feature story therein as if it were modernist fiction.

For the three years of this, Howard and Dorothy understood the juxtaposition of intimacy and parody as being their own little *post*modern statement. But as the quiet interlude between sex and scholarly shtick grew shorter and shorter, that understanding began to deconstruct *itself*.

This had been Howard's turn to fly, and they lay in Dorothy's bed in Berkeley. Their accustomed chuckling time quickly abated following his salacious close read of "Meet the Marriott Brothers." Quickly so in spite of their having laughed with somewhat more intense shared appreciation than usual.

They each rose from the bed. Having disrobed facing each other, they began to re-robe with backs to each other. They would next go to Peet's Coffee and talk shop. But before he could finish buttoning his shirt, she said, "Have you lately considered the joy of tenure?"

He finished the buttoning.

Then he turned, saying, "The joy simply abides, it seems to me."

She was dressed on this day—had greeted him at her door—in a white, pleated shirtwaist and dark skirt, as her Dorothy Richardson timelessly dressed while a starving teenager working in a New York artificial flower factory. She had dressed the same way on her last visit to Howard in Chicago as well, her current ongoing scholarly work focused as it was on an early-career memoir Dorothy R. had written of those years.

"Indeed," she said. "There are very few other joys of life that so reliably abide as tenure. Wouldn't you say?"

"I would," he said.

"For me," she said, "my redoubtable namesake is one such other joy."

"So I've gathered. And I see she still has gainful New York employment." At this he unfurled a gesture to her pleated shirtwaist with a hand that lately had fondled but had now quickly forgotten not just the feel but even the act of touching the tits therein.

"And your Hemingway is presently such a joy to you," she said. "These too abide. Through our research."

"Indeed."

"The details of which we are about to recount to each other at length."

He has begun to get her drift.

"As is our way," he said.

"As is our inevitable way."

"And as for our precious tenure," he said, "as both modernists, we are prohibitively redundant at each other's universities. Where our tenures are deeply rooted."

The truth of this had long been obvious to—if con-veniently ignored by—them both.

They each were aware of their own soft sigh now but not the other's.

"Our distance apart," Howard said, "might have kept it all fresh."

"One hoped," she said. "But instead we read to each other a thrice-a-year issue of our own personally tailored version of the *Journal of Modernism Studies*, covering the same specialty every time. Invariably. And for one not similarly obsessed, repetitively."

"And as for the other thing," Howard said, making the same gesture as a few moments ago but now indi-cating not the Richardsonian shirtwaist itself but the tits within and what they represent.

Which Dorothy instantly understood, saying, "Yes and yes and yes has become of course, of course, of course."

"Of course," he said.

"Yes," she said.

And so it was over.

❦

"How sad," Amanda says, even before Howard can lift his face from the screen.

Which he now does, his affect invisible.

She says, "You two seemed so right for each other."

"I presume you'd like to extend your writing day," he says.

"Yes I would," she says.

For both, disdain has turned decorum into sarcasm.

Though by the time Amanda sets herself up at the table

to write and Howard has slipped into his bed, the prickling of each has wearily diminished into something like indifference.

He can sleep.

She feels she can write from the place in herself she knows to write from.

April **2**, 2020

They sit down, as they have done eleven times before.

She is rested. She finished writing last night, before midnight.

They say nothing.

She looks at her screen.

For the first time since they began this project she is not content with what she's done.

Her writerly self suggests merely a misbegotten draft. All writers slam into that wall now and then. It's part of the process.

But it's not that simple.

It's an odd tale somehow.

Not bitchy not vengeful, but not apologetic not empathetic. For the record perhaps. But also broken off.

Just read it, she tells herself.
She begins.

౭ఞఞ

THE TWELFTH TALE
Amanda

His falsetto won me over. Oddly enough, since it prevailed against my motive for bringing Billy Jay Jessup to my hotel room in the first place, which would have been better served by my agreeing to his body while scorning the rest of him. But I even discounted the potentially mitigating thought that it was his drinking that fueled his transformation into a Dixie Chick behind the closed door of my bathroom.

"Cowboy take me away," he sang.

Which Billy Jay more or less did that night. Even though he was no more attuned to a woman and her body than my husband.

But to his credit he'd readily become a Chick in order to prepare for my bed.

A woman is used to such compromises.

This one happened to strike some kind of chord in me.

Perhaps because of Kathleen Higgins. He got to me by bending his gender. And he went on to teach me the Texas two-step, which even has a cuddle, and which we danced together at the Broken Spoke dance hall on my first visit to him in Austin after Howard moved out.

That particular struck-chord had its irony, however. It occasioned a reminder that I felt exclusively partial to the male part, in spite of how stupid it could be. And on that first night together, after we'd done our wrasslin', he'd even found it in himself not to continue onward to full drunkenness. A restraint that afterward seemed to endure in a readily tolerable, tipsy-only, halfway version. Endure at least during my six months of irreconcilable differences. In addition to my immediate Austin visit, Billy Jay did Chicago and together we did Cancun. They were pretty darn good.

Then on the early evening of the day when the judge signed the Judgment of Dissolution for my marriage, I was at the dormer desk of my third-floor writing room. I would soon begin renting Howard my half of our still jointly owned Evanston home. He was tenured not just to university but to city and I was strongly inclined to get away. I was free to write and publish and teach wherever I wished.

The sooner the better.

The part of me that wanted a quick—if nonbinding—next step to all this was still receptive to the cowboy.

I squared some papers on my desk.

The Eastern sky out my window was not yet dark, the lake made invisible by the tops of Orrington Avenue oak and maple.

And I thought of Billy Jay with the tops of Cancun beach palms outside our balcony doors backdropping his face, with us finished on the bed, and his eyes bigger and prettier than Martie Siedel's, the lead Dixie Chick a frame of reference because it had struck me at the time that I'd not heard him sing again in her voice since that first night with him. Nearly six months prior.

"Would you do me a favor?" I'd said.

"What's that, darlin'?" he'd said.

"You once sang in our bathroom. In Austin. A bit of 'Cowboy Take Me Away.' Can you do that for me now?"

His forehead crimped. His eyes too. "I did?"

"Sweetly."

"I've heard tell of this," he said.

"Heard tell?"

"About me. When the Tito's is right."

I let it go. Then and since.

And my Nokia rang now, there on my writing desk in Evanston. My snitch of a Nokia, as I'd come to call it over these past six months. Admiringly.

It rang a second time.

I answered.

"It's me," Billy Jay said. "Just me."

"Hello," I said. I would normally have said more. We knew how to talk, most of the time, Billy Jay and I. But his two words had a taint of something that I took a moment to try to assess. A faint imprecision in their speaking.

"This is your *big day*," he said.

"Yes," I said.

He had leaned in hard on the two words.

Then with a tone of elaboration he added, "Big big day. Big."

I said nothing.

Neither did he.

Until he abruptly declared, "I just *heard* that."

I didn't understand. He'd known this precise date was coming from its get-go.

And he clarified: "Heard *me*. Did I sound like something just now?"

Ah. "Something," I said.

"I need to be honest," he said.

"Are you drinking tonight, Billy?"

"Yes."

"Alone?"

"Yes."

"Because of my big day?"

"Not strictly," he said. And then, as if it were an afterthought, "Speaking."

"Not strictly speaking," I said.

"Right."

"The booze has its own way of talking," I said.

"And singing," he said.

He was somewhat past readily tolerable and tipsy-only. I understood.

"Now it's time for you to say it all," I said. "The reason you called."

"Ah."

"Honestly."

I sensed him struggling to think how to put it, given the Tito's count so far.

"May I?" I asked. "Say it for you?"

"Sure," he said. "I'm … you know."

"I do," I said. "My big day means I might be up for more time together, you and me. More often. And for longer. Which means you've got to show me what you're ready to show me tonight."

"I'm a drunk," he said.

"I figured as much," I said.

"I can't keep it together for you longer than I've been doing."

"Well then, git along little doggie." I said this with an alacrity that surprised me.

The brief silence on the other end of the line suggested a similar surprise.

But surely it was what he expected.

Be that as it may, a few more niceties followed—one part drunkenly maudlin, one part more or less relieved—and that was that.

We hung up.

The sky grew dark and I grew thoughtful about endings.

I had not heard from Howard. I had not expected to. Though he did not pass from me with alacrity, at least I felt no remorse.

By that and by the cowboy riding off into the sunset while having trouble sitting upright on his horse, I sorted out my priorities. With alacrity.

I picked up my phone and dialed.

☙❧

She stares at the screen for a long moment.

It does break off. She could have written on into the early morning and all day today. She didn't.

Howard waits.

Then he realizes. "That's it? A cliffhanger, is it?"

"The pieces wouldn't have fit together," she says.

He struggles now. There's a Howard in his head who wants to say *Your eye was on some other cowboy, was it? But he couldn't rustle up a cell phone signal out on the prairie?*

But the other Howard tries to read closely. He says, "There's a disconnected decade ahead of us in the overarching tale we're each telling. With only some transient characters. Maybe you're right to leave it at that."

This isn't what prompted her to stop, but about the few transients ahead, she agrees. "Then let's get our two interim histories out of the way right now," she says. "One exemplar each. In a couple dozen words or less. A synecdoche session."

"Good," Howard says. "Yes." And he says, "The divorced wife of a Northwestern mathematics professor. After his matrix of calculations, my book-talk seemed lush to her. Even sexual. But she almost never reads."

He folds his arms.

Amanda says, "The owner of an independent literary bookstore. He turned out to be a speed reader. Literally and metaphorically. Which isn't really *doing it* at all, in either realm."

Howard unfolds his arms.

"Not saying who," she says. "Don't ask."

"I wasn't going to."

"So we're done with all that? The years in between?"

"Yes."

"But you're still wondering," she says.

"The phone call that wouldn't fit the tale."

"I called Daniella."

Howard lifts his chin with an "Ah" of recognition.

"This was the time," she says.

"Yes, of course," he says. "Our Dani emerged to us."

"She did. I'd promised to call her on the day you and I were officially done. Spring semester was over. She was packing to come home."

"With the news about herself."

"Yes."

"It was Joanne Guinn from the start, wasn't it?" he says.

"It was. Though after Amherst they had a year apart. They needed that, having found each other so young."

Amanda and Howard fall silent now in their cross-back

side chairs before the balcony doors, their minds even tracking together for a time, about their daughter and her spouse actually turning forty later this year. And still happy with each other by all accounts.

Howard says, "So they're next in our story."

"Dani and Jo. Yes."

Amanda could elaborate. The words even pass briskly through her head: *If we are to stay together as a couple now—not that it's yet anything like a hope, but perhaps a whisper of a possibility—then a clue might reside in the way we got back together the last time.*

She does not speak them.

But he is already there. "Their wedding," he says.

"Their wedding."

"There are a lot of moving parts."

"You're right," she says. "Which ones we choose and what we say are important."

"Without the distortion of implicit debate."

"So again we both write until we're both done."

200

April **3–7**, 2020

The next morning they begin.

Howard opens his computer at the cleared table and he knows he will begin his tale with O'Hare, on the way to Boston, but before he writes a word he feels a little breath-grabbing upsurge of writerly well-being in the center of his chest.

At first it's simply about the freedom of neither having to anticipate a reply to the words he is about to write nor feel the onus of replying to the words he's lately heard from Amanda.

But that freedom releases a new thought. A thought, he realizes, that he's been shaping for a while. A thought that might, indeed, affect how he and Amanda hereafter conceive the remaining tales, how they execute them.

So he rises from his chair and approaches the closed bedroom door.

He knocks.

"What?" Amanda says. Not as sharply as he might have expected. Not that he was expecting anything but an invitation to open the door, as he is in the oblivious grip of an idea.

As it happens, she has replied to the interruption almost tolerantly.

Though he has already flung open the door.

And he proclaims, "It has occurred to me. These things we've been writing. They're not an assembly of tales. We get misled by the pieces seeming to talk to each other. These are novellas we're writing. In parallel but independent. I just thought you should know."

Amanda collects herself for a moment.

Given the part of herself she needs to access for this tale of a remarriage, she is ready to cut this man a little slack.

So she says, "You may be correct, Dr. Blevins. I have to say you've surprised me so far. An ornithologist flapping his arms and actually lifting off the ground. But please don't start scholarizing us now. You'll end up naming the bones in your own arms and instantly fall to the ground."

Howard straightens at this. Not as stiffly defensive a gesture as he would have expected. Almost attentive.

Which is just as well for both of them.

He is glad for the compliment buried in the admonition.

And he even recognizes the wisdom of the advice, though he also recognizes the truth of his analysis.

He says, "I shall fly away back to my computer now."

"Excellent," she says.

And he does.

℘

For five days and four nights they write with focused intensity, speaking little beyond practical necessities and commonplace courtesies in their mealtime and bedtime encounters.

Late morning on the fifth day, Amanda has been finished with her tale for a couple of hours already, and since she and Howard tend to stop for a bit of food around this hour anyway, she quietly opens the bedroom door and stands there.

Howard sits angled over his laptop, arms spread to either side, hands flat on the table, fingers drumming, his pondering posture while being *In the Zone*, as he has taken pleasure in calling it ever since Amanda acknowledged he was sounding like a "real writer."

She thinks to quietly step back into the bedroom, but Howard abruptly sits up straight and turns to her.

"Sorry," she says. "Not to rush you. I was just wondering."

"What time is it?" he says.

"Nearly noon."

"I'd rather not stop."

"Fine. I'd rather not eat."

"I'll be done in time for this evening," he says.

"Write on," she says.

Evening, April 7

And now it is evening and the balcony doors are open to the last hour of Paris spring sunlight.

Howard and Amanda suspect that between them they have words enough to carry them well into twilight.

Yes, it was high time for them to revisit these events. High enough that they begin now with no spoken words.

Howard opens his laptop.

❧❦

THE THIRTEENTH TALE
Howard

I had not laid eyes on my ex-wife in several years, knowing her to be—by way of Internet-fed curiosity—variously in California or Washington State or Florida, as she was a visiting nomad of a university creative writing teacher and a novelist with a following. But when I arrived at O'Hare Airport to head for Boston and our daughter's wedding, I found her sitting at the gate waiting for the same flight.

I jumped to the wrong conclusion.

As she read *The New Yorker* with her carry-on at her feet, before she even noticed me standing in front of her, my first words were, "So how long have you been back in Chicago?"

My reflex assumption being that she'd returned to the city as a home base long ago without letting me know.

Not that I cared.

I had not laid eyes on her in several years, after all.

My words startled her. The magazine fell to her lap and her face flashed upward.

"Sorry," I said.

She recovered at once, replying with snark: "You're sorry to think I live in Chicago?" Though she smiled a tolerant-seeming smile with it.

Which I ignored. Both snark and smile. "Sorry to startle you."

"About two hours," she said.

I was slow on the uptake, which she obviously read

on my face. With a head-pat of a tone she said, "How long I've been back."

"A connecting flight," I said, with an inner *Duh* and a twist of disappointment as I reinterpreted the smile I'd elicited a few moments ago as disdainful rather than tolerant. Thinking at once, *Not that I care. One way or the other.* "From somewhere exotic," I said.

"Hardly," she said. "I just drove down from Beloit."

"May I?" I nodded at the empty seat beside her.

"Of course."

I sat, saying, "Sorry. I'm feeling thick-headed. So. Exotic Wisconsin."

"There's nothing *thick* about your headedness," she said.

I was not particularly interested in her supplying an alternative adjective. I intervened, "Beloit College this time?"

"Just visiting. Teaching a workshop, fall semester. And you?"

"My visit begins its thirty-third year."

She turned her face from me. "Jesus."

And she kneaded a few moments at the silk neckerchief covering her throat, tied like a cowboy's.

What was in her head? I guessed at her thought: She and I had married just before that first fall semester at Northwestern.

Her hand came down.

But she remained thoughtful.

She took a breath and was beginning to bring her face back to me.

And I spoke from my guess: "We grow old."

Our eyes were now upon each other.

"We grow old," she said.

On the flight, Amanda sat a dozen rows in front of me, and at Logan Airport, after the long, slow, over-head-bag-impeded deplaning, I found she had gone on from the gate area. I presumed it was to baggage claim, where everyone from coach would inevitably spend time waiting, thus obviating any need to rush away.

Not that I care, I thought, methinking at once that I protest too much.

In the gaggle of travelers at the carousel it was Amanda who startled me, by appearing beside me as an unknown presence leaning suddenly into my arm and in a low-pitched voice saying, "I had to piss."

Obviously in explanation of her sudden disappear-ance at the gate.

I turned to her outsized eyes, and having been sep-arated from their discernment for nearly a decade, I was struck anew by how she could—not infrequently—read my mind. Through her gifts as a literary novelist, I dared say, but still.

"I figured as much," I said, just as low-pitched.

"Really?"

"I lived for more than two decades with you and your bladder," I said.

She laughed.

I had lied. About figuring as much. It was a lie I could thus make plausible. But no dramatic irony in all this. I knew from the get-go that I was lying. Not just about knowing she'd gone to piss. But about not giving a damn when I'd thought she'd rather go wait for her bag instead of walking with me.

And I gave all that a brief analytical assessment: *What*

the fucking hell?

From the back of my daughter's car, with my strapped seatbelt pressing insistently upon me and with the front seatbacks and headrests arrayed before me rendering the two women central to my previous adult life effectually invisible and with their rushing voices blurring from engine-and-road noise, I resisted the close read. *No metaphors for me, please.*

I held instead to a brief embrace of Dani a few minutes ago. Who had leapt from the driver's seat at the no-parking-no-standing loading curb of the terminal and circled her car and embraced her mother first, briefly, and then rushed to me and embraced me, as well.

She laid her head upon my chest and said, "Hey there."

It had been a while.

"Hey there," I said. Our long-standing reply.

I wanted to say more but I could not think what it might be. So I simply held her close and patted her on her back and fully experienced how inept I was being in that moment. Though in response she drew gently away, and when there was distance between us, she filled it by reaching back out to grasp each of my arms and give me a fine, firm shaking.

"So happy," she said.

"As am I," I said. As I was indeed.

Entering our hotel with mother and daughter, who were still absorbed with each other, I was the first to see Joanne across the lobby sitting in a stuffed chair, even as she first noticed us. She rose and began to stride our way.

She was dressed in her Boston lawyer garb, a tailored navy pantsuit that was a concession to no one but her own sense of herself. She had tied an impeccable Windsor knot on her crimson tie.

I had met her very briefly once before, here in Boston, and I'd liked her because I sensed her capable of exactly the moment she portrayed before me now: Approaching us, she glanced in the direction of her beloved and her beloved's mother, who were, it was clear, still unaware of her, and so without even a flicker of further attention in that direction, she turned her face to me and nodded once, sharply, flashing another fine thing I remembered about her, a collegially-warm, crooked smile.

I stepped to her approach.

We tightly thumb-crotched a handshake.

"Howard," she said.

"Counsellor," I said. "I have a hunch you're soon due in court."

She laughed.

She'd been clad in jeans and a pullover, though smart examples of both, when I'd met her before.

"Due," she said. "But not in court itself."

Now the clamored greetings of Amanda and Dani intervened with Joanne and drew her away, and I expected to be the odd one out from this point on. But Dani shortly broke off and stepped to me and said, "Jo's got to go soon. Why don't the two of you sit for a little while and catch up."

A couple of things were suddenly clear, from a close read: Amanda had already come to know Dani and Jo as a couple quite well over the years. And this *why don't the two of you* moment had been planned ahead of time.

I looked to Jo now, and though she was a few feet

away, closer to Amanda, she was watching Dani and me. Knowing what was being said, no doubt.

I looked back to my daughter. "Happy to," I said.

By the time I turned around, Jo was by my side. "Let's go get cushy over there," she said, taking my elbow to propel us toward the setting of lobby chairs where she'd been waiting.

When we settled in before each other, she said, "This is good. I'm just sorry we don't have more time. Not a hearing, but it's serious business."

"Serious I'm sure," I said. "Your firm's fighting the Defense of Marriage Act, isn't it?"

"It is. Big, good doings last month by a Federal District Court. Our firm's meeting in about an hour and a quarter with some of our counterparts from Sacramento who are fighting Prop 8. Comparing notes."

"Dani's proud of you," I said.

"Thank you," Jo said. "She appreciates your emotional support. As do I."

I nodded an *Of course*.

And we fell silent.

Here we were. Set up logically. Father of the spouse of the first part meeting the spouse of the second part with maybe half an hour to get to know each other, never previously having sufficient occasion to do so. The two of us being a lawyer and a literary scholar; a gay woman and a straight man; one who was, as I had been given to understand, a hell of a racquetball player, and one who occasionally enjoyed a certain prowess at tossing a sharply balled-up misbegotten page of a handwritten first draft of an academic paper into a trashcan sportingly kept at an eight-foot remove.

Not to mention our being a thousand miles apart.

There was distant merged laughter.

Both Jo and I turned our faces to it.

Dani and Amanda were moving toward the lobby lounge.

I watched my daughter hook her arm in the arm of her mother, but in my periphery I was also aware of Jo leaning toward me. She said, in a muted voice, "Dani and her mother are one of a kind."

I looked back to her.

She showed just a trace of that wry-seeming asymmetrical smile.

"I think you're right," I said.

"Dani's always been proud of you, too," she said.

That should have been an expected comment a short time ago. A courteous reflex thing, a routine thing, given my equivalent comment about Dani and her. But the gap in time, with Jo returning to the point well after the moment of reflex had passed, invested her words with actual sincerity.

I spoke now from my own reflex, driven, unfortunately, by a complex bit of impulsive quasi-reasoning. I said, "Pride goeth before divorce."

Jo laughed. Low, sharply. "Perhaps," she said. "But that's no more than to say, 'Marriage goeth before divorce.'"

In spite of her picking up the banter, I instantly knew to rebuke myself. I thrashed about in my head for a reason. And then I realized. A stupid little intellectual gag of a syllogism was at work: *Dani has always been proud of her father. Her pride-worthy father was divorced by her mother. Pride goeth before divorce.*

Particularly stupid because of this, which I quickly said, "Sorry. I didn't mean to cast a doubt on your imminent marriage."

Jo laughed out loud. "I'd be a poor lawyer if I didn't both see through and relish—and when necessary, exploit—locutions like that."

"Thanks," I said. "And I'm glad to hear of Dani's regard. I love her very much."

Jo leaned toward me and lowered her voice. "Love goeth before divorce," she said.

And we laughed together.

As the laugh subsided we kept our eyes on each other, my daughter's spouse-to-be and I. I liked her. "It's good to have at least a little one-on-one time," I said.

"Yes," she said. "It's not quite been put this way between Dani and me, but I got a sense that you and I would know how to talk to each other."

And I thought at once of her earlier observation: Dani and Amanda are one of a kind.

I took this in. There were corollaries to that. But with a touch of irony I let that settle on through to somewhere else in me. It invited some thought, but not for this moment.

The thinking I preferred to do for the moment was with the thoughtful woman before me.

"So tell me, counselor," I said. "How do you make reason prevail in a courtroom where your opponent's case is contrived by emotion? Especially the malignant emotions of a politically schizophrenic twenty-first century America?"

"They're called judges," she said. "And juries."

"And when those succumb to the specious and the basely persuasive?"

"That's called the human condition."

"Oh, that," I said. "That's the land my discipline dwells in."

"So you do," she said. "But you dwell there to bring reason to the courtroom of scholarship. Yes? "

I chuckled an assent.

And she went on: "The exegesis of farts and corpse gas and women's butt holes?"

Now I laughed aloud. "You've read Joyce?"

"I have," she said. "And I understand your case for his seriousness, professor. I just think he is often full of the shit he seriously tries to exalt."

We spoke for a time of James Joyce and the close read of literary texts and then we circled back—somehow quite naturally—to California's Proposition 8 and the close read of law and of Conservative screed. And in all of this, the parts of our brains and the parts of our sensibility fit neatly together, this woman-spouse of my daughter and me.

And so, in a brief pause in our conversation, during which she discreetly looked at her watch, I asked, "Do you have to go now?"

"Ah, sorry you noticed the glance."

"I understand the need."

"Because I'm enjoying our chat."

"I am too," I said. "I suspect it's the only chance we'll have."

"You're probably right. For this visit certainly. So let me stretch it a few more minutes."

"Are you sure?"

"Yes."

"Good," I said. "Because a question has been growing in me that you're excellently suited to answer."

"Shoot," she said.

"You earlier observed that your wife and my wife are one of a kind."

I paused only very briefly, for effect. For emphasis.

Jo instantly expanded: "In mind and in sensibility."

"Yes," I said. "Exactly. And it seemed to me from the evidence of just this past half hour that you and I could well be described the same way."

"And from what Dani says of you," she said. "Yes. Simply working in different disciplines."

I nodded at this, then said, "And I take it that tomorrow is a formality, a sweet one but a formality for the two of you."

"You take it correctly. Dani and I have lived together for nearly a decade."

After these preliminaries, I found myself without immediate adequate words. The question had been growing in me for a long while, though Jo's rare qualifications to answer it had greatly hastened its asking.

But I was thrashing to phrase it. She was waiting. I at least had to start: "So the two one-of-a-kind pairs we just identified. Mind and sensibility seem like an awful lot. Seem pretty comprehensive."

I stop.

I was feeling a little stupid. The question should have been clear.

Jo was looking at me as if she sensed those two things going through my head and she was in agreement.

And abruptly I understood the resistance. Partly I was averse to oversimplification. Partly I was afraid to sound as if I were calling into question the marriage of my daughter and this estimable woman.

But I wanted to hear her answer. Needed to.

"The growing question," I said and paused.

"Yes?" she said.

"Your discipline is better with questions. I'm better at inferences."

"All right," Jo said. "What pairing are you actually interested in?"

"Amanda and me."

"How would you describe that pair in terms of mind and sensibility?"

"*Not* one of a kind," I said.

"And how does that difference make you feel?"

"It's complicated."

"To express?"

"To live," I said. "And therefore to express, here, extemporaneously, yes."

"Then let me ask this," she said. "Did that difference have a significant impact on your marriage?"

And I answered at once: "How could it not?"

We were silent for a moment.

Jo bent near and said, low, "Is that a yes?"

"Yes."

She nodded a little. Tight of lips but sympathetically wide of eyes. Then she said, still low, "So what is your question?"

I saw a way forward now.

"You and Dani are different in the same way. A difference lived-with for a decade. How have *you* two figured it out?"

Jo sat back in her chair, rested her elbows, intertwined her fingers, set her chin there. And she furled her brow to consider an answer for a long moment.

Finally, she lifted her chin and released her hands to

the chair's armrests. She said, "It might be that the best answer requires the very qualities that our women share. But what you and I share is adept at translation."

"I appreciate that."

"Differences can obviously be off-putting. Deeply so. But they can be charming. They can be stimulating. In principle they can. And if you get married in the first place, obviously the engaging stuff was there at some point. And you were married how long?"

"Twenty-two years."

"And divorced?"

"Almost ten."

"If the question still presses on you, how to make that work, some measure of engagement remains. In an enduring way."

She fell silent. Thinking a bit. Her reasoning was sound. I recognized and respected and shared her mind's process. And so I feared her final glance at her watch. I said, "You're doing great by the reckoning of my similar mind." I held up my own left wrist. "Forgive me for pressing you. But can you translate the last bit of your answer? Before you have to go?"

She nodded. But it was with a bit of a sideways head tilt. And a bit of a compression of her lips. Not encouraging. And she said, "This has all been impromptu. And when a thing comes up in court that you don't expect, but you need to find your way forward to a smart and focused thing, you do the logical set up first. Speak your own process, as it were."

"Like just now," I said.

"Like just now," she said.

"Like the previous bits," I said.

"Which made you lift your wrist at me."

"Have you delayed enough?"

"The answer I keep coming back to is derived from Dani and me."

"Naturally," I said.

"So there might not be a solution attached. If that's what you're seeking."

"Then call it an explanation."

"Okay. Mind and sensibility. That's just two of the three horses in the troika."

"The third being the body," I said.

"The body," she said. "If two of the three are largely different in a couple, there are ways for that to work. Even potentially thrive. By charm and stimulation. But if all three require the reconciling of opposites, I keep thinking that's the problem. I suspect any two of the three are capable of working. But if your mind is rigorous to your spouse's intuitive, if your emotions are tempered to your spouse's unfettered, then your bodies would have to be in lovely accordance to make the differences captivating. One of the three has to be congruous."

I sat back in my chair.

I thought: *How does that sound somehow true? She's a lawyer, after all, is how. If she has sketchy evidence or a guilty client to work with and is going to be persuasive, she has to be arrestingly specious.*

"Interestingly argued," I said. "I will need to deliberate on that."

"I hope I'm wrong, if need be," she said. And then: "Your daughter would love to see her parents reconnected."

I willed a knowing nod. To mask my surprise. I knew Dani loved us both. But this had never fully occurred to me.

Jo rose.

I rose.

"I greatly enjoyed this," I said.

"So say we all," she said.

"Don't you miss her?" Dani asked me, almost first thing, as we sat, just the two of us, in the lobby lounge late that same afternoon. Meaning Amanda.

"It's been a long while," I said.

"That makes it a good test. Even a moderate amount of missing would be significant after all this time. "

It was clear she was going to push this. I hadn't had a chance to think it out since Jo sprung it on me a few hours ago. "A long while," I repeated, lamely.

"Going on ten years," she said. "So do you?"

"You've kept count."

"Automatically. The year after you moved out, Jo moved in."

"Jo says you have hopes about your mother and me."

"Does she?"

"Damn," I said. "Did I break a confidence?"

"No. It's okay. I freely admit it."

"She's most excellent, by the way. Your Jo."

"Yes, she is. You're being evasive."

I shrugged.

With a wee eyebrow-lifted head-dip, she said, "Which suggests to me there's something at least moderate still stirring around in you."

"Not stirring."

"Residing."

"Lurking maybe." I gave her this concession to stop the interrogation. And maybe even did so, I told myself, out of honesty. Sure. Lurking. But this was my ardent darling daughter, and for her deliberative Jo to have brought all this up and used the word *love* to describe my daughter's longing, I found myself lapel-shaken to reconsider. The diminishment to *lurking* was not so much a strategic concession but a self-deceptive inaccuracy. *Residing* was, in fact, closer to it. And with that came another, even more surprising thought: In the last few hours, maybe the accurate word was not too far distant from *stirring*.

All of which flashed through me without a suggestion for an appropriate clarification. Much less an actionable solution.

"I'll take lurking," Dani said.

I did not quibble.

Instead, in as firm a tone of voice as I could muster while remaining gentle, I pressed for a change of subject. "So what else is happening in your life, my darling daughter?"

She let me get away with that, using the prompt to talk passionately about her little storefront art gallery on one of the narrow, hilly streets near the Massachusetts State House and about the artists she represented. I listened enough to ask a reasonable aesthetic question now and then, for which she had smart answers, but as we talked I was mostly appreciating her moving on in this sweet conversational concession to me. Which made me feel bad about brushing off her surprising longing for her decade-divorced parents to reunite; which made me open myself to such an idea and begin to recognize the previously overlooked but perhaps not inconsiderable pieces of the marriage left in me. All of which struck me as smart rhetorical strategy on her part to put me in this very frame of mind, which made me wonder if Dani had received some wise counsel on the matter from the canny lawyer she loved. Not that that suspicion undermined the strategy. Indeed, since such advice would've been sought, not volunteered, it even reinforced my growing consciousness of the depth of Dani's longing, no matter how odd it might have seemed to me.

So when Dani paused as if there were no more about the gallery, I said, "Did you ask the equivalent question of your mother?"

In spite of a good deal of unrelated talk intervening, she knew at once what I was asking. *Don't you miss him.* "I did," she said.

She paused again. Similarly.

"And?" I said.

"Cagey as you," she said.

"Good for her," I said.

"You two are one of a kind," she said.

I laughed out loud at this.

So there we all were at the Boston Public Library, in the McKim wing that comprised the original building of 1895, in what was now called the Abbey Room, which was of moderate size, modeled upon a room in the library in the palace of the Doge of Venice.

A hundred of us sat upon Renaissance replica chairs. Assorted nearest of kin were in the first row, I on one side of a middle aisle and Amanda on the other, by our instinctive own choice. We all faced shuttered windows, where a Unitarian minister stood, a woman in black robe and rainbow stole.

Before her were my daughter in a white dress and her intended in a black tuxedo. The couple had already turned to face the minister, who was beginning to speak.

Of course the scene now underway before me was not just the formalizing rationale but the happy raison d'être of our gathering. But the words being spoken were far from fittingly inspired, even making a secularist scholar grudgingly wistful for *The Book of Common Prayer.*

And so my attention drifted.

But I had been set up for this.

When I'd first entered this space, I'd become immediately interested in the fifteen massive canvas panels that high-up encircled the room in Pre-Raphaelite hyper-realism, the creation of a prominent American illustrator, the eponymous Edwin Austin Abbey. They comprised a story montage portraying the quest for the Holy Grail undertaken by Sir Galahad, clad in a red robe of purity in each panel. No less a seminal modernist figure than Henry James wrote a detailed description of each of these very paintings that was published in a handbook by the library in 1914.

Flanking the windows and the ongoing wedding ceremony were two scenes. To the left, in a boat upon a sea, Galahad kneels before an angel who sits in the prow, holding the Grail, bearing it to the mystical island of Sarras near Egypt.

On the right was the final painting of the series.

And this one baffled the hell out of me.

Galahad is kneeling again, this time before a company of half a dozen fresh-faced female angels in white gowns bedecked in golden vines and leaves. In the center of them stands a figure in a white robe with arms raised high and hands turned inward. But they hold nothing directly. In the space between these hands floats the Holy Grail in the air.

But baffled, yes. And the more I would later learn, the more baffled I became. All of it regarding the face and head of this figure. The robe had a raised hood, but the head and face were almost entirely visible. As did *every* other commentator on the Abbey paintings before or after, Henry James identified the figure as Joseph of Arimathea, the rich man and secret follower of Christ who purchased the chalice of the Last Supper from Pontius Pilate. He was portrayed in artwork for centuries, unfailingly, as an old man with a long beard. So in the culminating painting it was logical for this to be holy Saint Joe.

But. While my daughter got married I carefully stared at, scrutinized, meticulously parsed the parts of this head and face.

Several redundant times.

The undetailed blocks of color were simplified, but their shapes and color were unambiguously representational. And I could come to only one conclusion: It was the head and face—and even a bit of the throat—of a cat.

Saint Joseph was a cat. A black house cat with a white muzzle. Rendered in—dared I to think it?—a proto-modernist gesture.

I had to suppress an immediate outright bark—or perhaps mew—of recognition.

Even with later close examination of the Holy Grail paintings I would find no such subversive touch in any of the others. It was clear to me that this Edwin Abbey—whose overt art was masterfully meticulous in rendering the minute details of the physical world—had a covert vision of the universe. *Abbey's* God—in the very moment of having His special saint release to Heaven a major relic of His putative Son—was foreshadowing His plan to restructure belief for a *modern* twentieth century.

And now my daughter and the woman she had just married were kissing and the room was sighing.

I figured Edwin Abbey's modernist God was still at Their transformative work.

Joanne and Daniella kissed lingeringly in the Abbey Room.

෧ᢀᢀ᠖

At once within Amanda: *A lot of moving parts indeed, in your Boston wedding tale. Thanks mostly to Jo. But it's your inert parts that yet again shout to me. Saint Joseph of Arimathea portrayed with the head of a cat by a crypto-proto-modernist hyper-realist painter. Thoroughly analyzed even while our daughter kisses her new wife. Holy fuck, Howard. And the dancing. With no deadline on your writing and with our personal mandate in Paris, you don't even go onward to that. You think you can do this literary writing thing, Professor? You averted your eyes, Dr. Headupyourbutt.*

But she does not speak.

From her own tale, from its own climax, she knows there was some other part of Jo's troika trying to pull its weight in Howard. Still.

But the Pietà was worse, really. She didn't challenge him on that either.

I should have.

Through this rush of feelings in Amanda, Howard has been gazing at his computer screen, at the tale he has just told.

She reads him now, in her own way.

His gaze is unmoving, as if focused on a pixel, as if the actual screen he is reading is in his head. And yet he does so with an ease about him, a little bit wide-eyed with an almost smile that registers on her as tenderness.

Which surprises her.

How is she to assess all this?

Her own tale that awaits has its clues.

Howard begins to lift his face to her.

She lowers hers, briefly closes her eyes, wags her head. *Let him see that, at least. Let him close-read that.*

Then she opens her computer.

She begins.

ঌৄৎঌ

THE FOURTEENTH TALE
Amanda

Their lips touched.

My daughter's lips and the lips of the woman she loved.

In the Boston Public Library. In a room that was there from the beginning, from 1895, the Abbey, with dark oak paneling and a beamed ceiling and a French Rouge marble fireplace. A room conceived and constructed in a world that would damn this kiss.

But here and now, even vows of marriage have been spoken.

Jo first. And then Dani. Each concluding, *For all the days of my life.*

And now this kiss.

The three of us had spent some time together through their cohabiting years, but this was the first truly serious kiss I'd witnessed between them. They had always been fastidious before me, though I understood from my daughter, privately, that Jo was quite persuasively full in the expression of her love *in camera*. Dani had laughed softly as she used the legal term to reassure me of their passion, sharing an ongoing joke between herself and her crackerjack of a lawyer lover.

But this public moment *in bibliotheca* was serious.

Not just in the *fuck-you* to the room and the values that resided in its conception. More importantly serious in the kiss itself.

Their lips overlapped, deeply, but paused then, speaking thus of the decade they'd been together, a vision of what a decade—or even two—could evolve to when two people were in love and committed. A kiss of deep touching made even more natural, more at peace in the touching, *more* connected not less, from the passing of years.

Yes, I thought, as if crying aloud to them.

Yes.

So much was in me at that moment. Composted there.

Such as the day of the dissolution of a marriage where I myself had made vows *for all the days of my life* or perhaps *till death do us part* or perhaps *for* or *till* or *as long as* some similar thing, a thing I could not precisely remember now in the Abbey Room of the Boston Public Library nor had I remembered even in the Writing Room of the Amanda Duval Evanston House on the day of the dissolution of that marriage.

I watched the sky go dark over the treetops of oak and maple on Orrington Avenue on that day, and I picked up my phone and dialed my daughter.

"Mama," she answered.

"It's done," I said.

"I assumed," she said. "How are you?"

"Good."

"Does it still feel right?"

I knew she regretted the divorce. We'd spoken of it. "Irreconcilable differences" was adequate for the courts but not for an only child who loved both her parents. Even when elaborated upon—with, ironically, an abstract persuasiveness—as a worldview divide between artist and scholar.

"Trust me," I said now.

"Of course," she said.

"We've spoken of it enough these past few months, my darling. Yes?"

"I'm packing today," she said.

Her junior year at Amherst was over. So, obviously, was our conversation about the divorce.

"I've decided," she said.

I knew what she meant.

"Jo will be with me," she said.

"Didn't she want a permanent decision before coming along?"

"She did," Dani said. "She got one."

"So you've answered the question?"

"Whether I'm a lesbian? Probably. But I was asking the wrong question, Mama. It's not a generic one. The question I had to answer was: Do Joanne Marie Guinn and I fit harmoniously together—even if complexly—and is that potentially forever? Which is a question concerning two specific individuals. Come to think of it, *even if complexly* is wrongheaded. I should say *moreover, com-*

plexly. Complex harmony may well be a *necessity* for forever."

On the day it formally ended, I heard Dani addressing my own marriage. For which she clearly had full subtextual intention.

She thus commenced what would become, for the following nine years, a usually set-aside but never completely abandoned motif between us.

And now she was kissing her wife.

A hand took mine and squeezed it.

It belonged to Jo's mother, who was sitting next to me in the front row.

Her husband was not with her. He had repudiated his daughter's action.

Guinn was this woman's maiden name, formally taken on by Jo as her first act upon passing the bar. The mother was still married to and living with that man and with his name.

I returned the squeeze.

Jo and I had sat down yesterday afternoon in the Marriott's second-floor lobby lounge to chat for a while. We looked out across a convergence of two streets to the wing of the library where our daughters were to marry. Jo had met Howard here a couple of hours before. Just before this meeting, Dani made a chirpy, emphatic point to me that her fiancée had hit it off with her father very nicely indeed, saying, "I knew she would. I'm so glad."

"So you liked my ex?" I asked Jo. Rhetorically. Pretty much straightaway. That actually surprised me more than it did her. Indeed, she seemed not at all surprised. As for me, I heard my own tone in the asking, and I was relieved that it seemed friendly, light-hearted, even amused. As for my surprise, in the half dozen or so conversations I'd had with Jo over these past several years, they were always during limited, passing-through visits and always with Dani attached to the conversation. Jo and I had never spoken a word that I could recall about Howard. In spite of this matter having been at least somewhere in Dani's mind all that time. But around Jo, the matter had been carefully avoided.

So I was not sure what prompted me to bring it up with her now, one-on-one. Especially with this seeming urgency.

I thought: *Perhaps my regard for the formality of marriage runs deeper than I realized, with Jo the shortly-to-be-wife suddenly empowered to care about this.*

Then there was my own curiosity, if not concern, about the potential corollary. That all three of them were of the same mind about me. Thinking I'd blundered in the break up.

Not that they knew what I knew. Or what—at that time or even at the time of the wedding—I *thought* I knew.

"Yes," Jo said. "I liked your ex."

"Why is that?"

"The woman I'm marrying tomorrow likes him."

Still another surprise: I was disappointed in the explanation. I respected Jo. I realized I was trying to ask her to explain her regard for Howard.

How to do that indirectly?

I had no inspiration.

So a thought came to me.

Yes, a thought.

I said, "And that woman you're marrying. If she were, instead, the very image of him, if her mind and sensibility made her obviously her father's child, would you still be marrying her?"

Jo leaned back against her chair.

I was sorry I'd said it.

I had a surge of fear.

Which was at once heightened, as Jo laughed a little. Knowingly? As if there were, in fact, presently points of contention similar to Dani's mother and father? Was I stirring something up?

"Of course I would still marry her," she said.

An answer which did me no good. Jo herself being the equivalent of Howard in their marriage. Which served me right for trying to *think* this through.

She added, with a gentle laugh, "Though I might just nudge her toward law school and a joint practice."

All right, I thought. *Let it go.*

But she understood, saw through me, this lawyer, this woman, my daughter's soon-to-be wife. She leaned forward and offered me her hand.

I reached across the table and took it.

She said, in almost a whisper, "You're not actually asking if I think *likes* can attract, are you?"

"No."

"Has Dani told you about her complexity theory?"

"She has. She treasures the complex harmony of the two of you."

"She's right about us," Jo said, softly. "For a woman of the heart, she's got a good idea there."

"And she's grateful for you," I said.

Instead of remarking: *If one can pull it off.*

An image of the possible success of which, however, was the just-married kiss in the Boston Public Library.

It ended with both of them gently pulling away at what seemed to be precisely the same moment without any apparent signal preceding from one or the other, no slight movement of a shoulder, no small intake of breath, no sigh, nothing. Just the elegant synchronization of these two women who had loved each other for a decade already.

They were grateful for each other. These two specific, complex individuals.

Now the two of them stood beneath the vaulted, terracotta ceiling of another nineteenth-century room in the Boston Public Library, the Guastavino. We had all dined at tables at one end of the room and the food was laid out at the other. The large center space was open for dancing and the newlyweds had appeared there just as a string quartet in tuxedos began to play Strauss the Younger's "The Blue Danube."

We all rose from the tables and crowded forward and cheered them.

Dani was form-fittingly dressed in white with a strapless scoop bodice, though she was covered upward to the throat in sheer lace that bloomed onto her shoulders and arms as flute sleeves of flowers. My girl. And her girl was a dapper dandy in black tuxedo with satin peak lapels, black satin side stripes, and a white bow tie on her pleated-front white shirt.

They bowed to the cheers.

What moved me to look toward Howard at that moment? Even as I clapped? He'd come from our round table of ten but most of the others from there had gathered between us.

He was applauding as well but had the same impulse. He turned his face to me.

This was our daughter before us, after all. He and I had been married for more than two decades. Nearly a full decade later we were each now alone in our lives, a fact we had learned in some unmemorably offhand way sometime in the last twenty-four hours, at the airport perhaps. Not that it mattered.

Now he simply turned his face to me, and we nodded and looked away.

As our daughter and her wife began to waltz.

The piece began with a languorous introduction and our couple was showing their clearly refined ballroom skills, doing the steps of the Viennese waltz, meticulously so at this briefly slower tempo, Jo upright and leading and Dani with head and shoulders gracefully thrown back. Then the musicians picked up the pace and Dani and Jo did likewise, gliding in onward-flowing clockwise circles in a great arc around the floor, and as the arc passed the quartet of musicians, Jo adjusted the circle with a back-step into a reverse turn and a renewal of the circle counterclockwise, and they flowed on until they reversed again, and all the while they were looking face-liftedly away from each other in stylized ease, as if they were supremely certain of each other's feelings, which they clearly were to the delight of all of us who watched, and at last this familiar music seemed about to segue into a classic ballroom waltz.

But instead the quartet did its own reverse turn—a lift of notes and the briefest of pauses—and the tempo throttled down and the music glided forward a century from Strauss to Victor Young, from "The Blue Danube" to "When I Fall in Love." Jo pulled Dani close and Dani laid her head on Jo's chest and they began a body-blended, tempo-oblivious, personal variation of a sock-hop box step.

The crowd collectively swooned, and after a few more bars of dancing, our couple separated from their full-body embrace just enough to free one arm each and do a box-step circle while waving for the crowd to join them on the floor.

Which many did at once.

I stayed standing where I was as Jo and Dani pressed their bodies together once more, and I watched them turn this simple dance of my teenage years into something elegant, watched them loving each other—for a long while already, and for this special moment, and for what clearly felt like a legitimate shot at forever.

I watched them till the other dancers obscured them.

While I thought of a man.

Not the obvious one, even to rue. I thought of Nat King Cole. Inextricably part of this particular song for a girl who came of age in the late Fifties and early Sixties. I heard his voice in my head, singing of love forever, and that held me until the song was over and the string quartet took up Billy Joel.

How typical of Jo and Dani this all suddenly seemed, programming songs that induced us to fill our own heads with pop musical words but riding the instrumental current of a classically chamber sound. And the sentiment that carried us now in our heads was "Just the Way You Are."

But almost at once Jo and Dani emerged from the dancing crowd, heading our way, holding hands briefly and then letting go, Jo angling toward me and Dani angling the other way, toward her father.

Jo stepped close and took my right hand in her left and put her other low on my back, holding me as if to lead, while keeping a mother-daughter upper-arm distance between us. I let her.

"Shall we?" she said.

"We shall," I said. "Not incidentally, you two are beautiful together."

"Thank you. I'm very happy to dance now with my new mother."

So we swirled away with Jo leading us sweetly and commandingly, and by the end of the song's second verse her expert dance steps had brought the two of us quite near another dancing couple, Dani and Howard.

Which, of course, had been her plan. Or at least a core part of it, if not the whole of it, as Jo has read my mind, saying, "I truly did enjoy dancing with you, Amanda. Let's do it just for us a little later."

And she let me go, even as Dani was letting go of her father, and the two newlyweds gently pushed Howard and me into each other's arms.

I was surprised at the outcome but more surprised that my body's reflex was immediately to accept it. Moreover: Howard's eyes engaged mine and quickly shifted away, as did mine, to Dani and Jo embracing into their dancing couplehood, and then both our gazes returned to each other at once, uncomplainingly. Yes, he accepted this as well.

Accepted what, exactly? Big deal, right? Of course we might dance together at our daughter's wedding.

Which we began to do, holding our joined hands aloft, my other on his shoulder, his other around me and low on my back, though with him keeping an ex-husband upper-arm distance between us.

Still, we danced.

We remained on the fringe of the other dancers.

"They looked lovely together," he said, drawing a little closer to speak into my ear through the music.

"They did," I said, leaning upward to his.

"Are we for show here, them arranging us into each other's arms?"

"More than show. You know Dani. She has never let go of her hope."

"Intended persuasion," he said, ponderingly.

As I thought: *But does she somehow know us?*

I decided at once not to speak this.

And that decision was barely made when Howard said, "Maybe she knows us better than we do."

It had been almost ten years.

I'd had no one else. Not even close, really. Nor had he, as it would turn out.

As we danced at our daughter's wedding, we still accepted each other's mask of irreconcilable differences, still knowing only a partial truth behind our own. As for me: I had fucked the cowboy but only because I thought Howard was about to do likewise with a fellow scholar. While at the same time, unbeknownst to me, he had only *nearly* fucked a woman who revered him for the part of him that often alienated me, though he never suspected anything about his wife.

He was right about my alienation; I was right about his intentions, delayed though they were till we split up.

As we danced, without the fuller story of each other, my perceptions of him and of my own past actions were the greater impediment to Dani's hope.

But there was once something between Howard and

me. Something that had been worth a substantial number of years. Though I had not consciously sought such a reminder, I realized that what once connected us had persisted despite our sometimes tumultuous differences. A connection deeply rooted in our complex shared devotion to literary creation. So complex that the tumult of it was as much personal as it was aesthetic.

I thought: *Perhaps something in my self, even beyond the writer, had persistently wanted to be worthy of serious thought, and something in his self, beyond the scholar, had persistently wanted to live the feelings he analyzed. We each felt safest in our primary self but were conscious of our other. After all, that polarity comes together as it bears upon the great and eternal question that resides in all works of literature: Who the fuck am I?*

And yes, all of that thought was *me* doing the analyzing, which was why, to clear my head, my hand moved a little farther up his arm and then curved behind his shoulder. If we were to dance, I wanted it to be truly *me* doing it.

And he pulled me closer to him.

We'd had a brief one-on-one conversation at the airport in Chicago. I'd come down from Wisconsin that morning, where I was teaching. We exchanged small talk that at some point prompted us to agree that we were both getting old and at some later point devolved into a silence more comfortable than awkward, until it was time to board the plane.

I said to him now, "I'm sorry we didn't talk more at O'Hare. I was weary from the early drive."

"I understand," he said.

"I was a bit testy too, I'm afraid. At the airport."

"Not at all," he said. Almost ardently.

"We missed a chance to get caught up a bit," I said.

"My part would've been very familiar," he said.

I thrashed a bit in my mind to find a way to dispute him. I couldn't. What I actually felt surprised me. A feeling not unrelated, I realized, to our getting old: *There are joys in the familiar.*

But for some reason I was not prepared to say this to him.

"Your part surely would've had the new in it," he said.

"One would think," I said. In a tone that he did not have to read very closely to hear as a weary disclaimer.

All this we were speaking in stage whispers to be heard over the string quartet.

I pressed gently on him with my hand behind his shoulder.

He felt it as I intended it—*Let's just dance now*—for he pulled me even closer to him and picked up the tempo of our box-stepping, which our talk had dragged down to something like largo.

And then, with my attention fully on my ex-husband holding me close for the first time since I could not remember when, we did a little turn and our bodies moved a bit across each other, and it was quite clear to my right hip that Howard had a boner.

ॐॐॐ

Howard, Howard, Howard, she thinks.

Now that she has read her tale aloud, Amanda is aware that she, too, is staring unmoving at her screen, as he had been. And just as she implied in him in her tale, she feels something akin to tenderness.

Howard, Howard, Howard.

Even her head-wagging after his tale—over his distracted-ness at his daughter's wedding—begins to revise itself.

That boner of his followed all that and was the inciting incident for this second marriage of ours.

And as workshop terminology has crept into her thinking, a classic example slips in with it: Romeo's first glance across the ballroom to Juliet. Like the moment with Howard, a small thing that incites a large story.

She smiles a bit now: *No insult intended, Howie. Small compared only to the size of the story it precipitated.*

And her tenderness asserts itself. About Howard's body. Pre-sexual in this envisioning, the body of the still sixteen-year-old high-schooler off to the Yale Summer Session, his gifted mind out yearning into his future and his already displaced, body-root-ed feelings about to be extracted and bottled and set upon his mother's makeup table.

His vast shadow of a mother. A likely suicide. Perhaps even recogniz-ably so. Of course *he'd try to relocate forever to his keenly rational mind for an enduring refuge.*

Meanwhile Howard ponders his long-ago erection. Ponders it unto a ponderousness of the keenly rational variety. But this includes his being aware of the process going on within him. Which prompts him to willfully turn his focus outward to Amanda, who fell silent upon invoking the state of his penis a decade ago and is still looking slightly downward, at her com-puter screen.

And he close-reads her as he would to fully comprehend a literary text: Her gaze—obviously in lingering response to that very invocation—her gaze is unblinkingly fixed and a little bit wide-eyed, and playing about her mouth is a faint smile that registers on him, with a slight shock, as tenderness. Shocking enough, however, that he tries at once to derive from it a theme, a thought, a trope, a vision.

He fails.

A failure he also takes note of, and since Amanda's face rises fully now from her screen and her eyes fix on his, he asks, "So you noticed my …"

His pause for a word is less than a single breath long, but Amanda hears the pause and expects an academic, even a clinical alternative of a word for *boner*. A corresponding expectation is unconscious—that his choice will thus taint her presently lingering tenderness for him.

"… foreshadowing," he says.

And she sits with this a moment. Relieved. Untouched by taint.

"Nice word," she says. And she means it. Yes, a working term in plot pedagogy. But one she has always liked. How it carries a sensually impactful imbedded metaphor. And his use of it was unexpected in this context. Nuanced.

"Thank you," he says.

"So in that moment," she says, "did you yourself sense the foreshadow of your cock?"

She regrets her word-choice of *cock* even as it comes out of her mouth. She chides herself: *I liked his alternate word for boner but it was still a euphemism. I didn't reassert bluntness in a sarcastic way, but to his ear it surely registered as just the sort of banter-masked verbal rough stuff that over the past nine years has helped lead us to this Paris apartment.*

But Amanda's concern is mistaken in this case. She does not fully understand the featured body part itself in her bantered bluntness, nor its nuanced relationship to its owner. Particularly when it was doing what a man of the mind would reasonably hope it *would* do when called upon.

He is fine.

Which allows him now to sound more like his comfortable self. He says of his boner, "It's the nature of foreshadowing to be a mere *shadow* indeed, whose recognizable shape will not be clear until later. Did I foresee the two of us in bed on that very night? Hardly."

Hearing her comfortably thoughtful Howard, she feels a sigh come upon her, which she suppresses to a barely audible exhalation.

And she says, "If we're serious about this place we've come to …"

She pauses.

He waits.

She still hesitates.

"Do you mean that as a question?" he asks.

"I suppose I do. There's more that I intended, but I suppose I'd like an answer first."

"Then yes," he says. "We are serious. About why we are here."

"If so," she says, "we each need to write a tale of that night."

He begins to consider this. But without thought, he knows.

"Yes," he says.

"And again we write …"

"Yes," he says. "Simultaneously. We must slip into that bed together."

April 8, 2020

Both sets of hands poise over their keyboards on the following morning. Poise and linger and fall and rise and poise again as Howard and Amanda face the challenge they so glibly took up for themselves the night before.

But each soon finds the place within them that they've learned to write from in the past three weeks. By late that afternoon—at the approximate time when the writer presenting that day would potentially initiate a pause for dinner, a time when they both knew to pause if they were writing simultaneously—neither of them looks up from their screen or lifts their hands from their keyboard.

They write on, until the afternoon passes and the evening light of Paris in the spring begins to wane.

Finally, Howard saves his work, closes his MacBook cover, and rises from the table.

He feels faintly disoriented.

The apartment has gone dim.

He looks at his watch and winces slightly in surprise.

It is 8:05.

He crosses to the bedroom door. He knocks.

"Yes?" her voice replies.

He opens the door, and Amanda, propped and stretched for writing on the bed, looks up from her computer.

She too seems a bit disoriented.

"We've gone on and on," Howard says.

"We have," she says.

"Believe it or not, I'm already done," he says.

"In ten minutes or so, me too."

"Given our topic, our briskness might seem a criticism of my performance," he says.

She laughs.

He joins her.

"Not at all, as a matter of fact," she says.

"I'm glad to hear it," he says.

And so, twenty minutes later, they eat a bit of food, though in silence, knowing the next words that need be heard reside in their computers.

Then they carry the cross-back chairs to the reading space before the balcony doors.

"Who shall begin?" Howard asks.

"Please," Amanda says, motioning with a slow-flaring hand to the center of his chest.

꙳

THE FIFTEENTH TALE
Howard

How long had it been since I danced with a woman?
I was holding Amanda now.

I'd held a few women since her. But not to dance.

I had no memory of my last dance with her. Was it in Paris, when we met again at Shakespeare and Company, when this Billy Joel song was new? When her first novel was new? When she smelled of the woods? Smelled of the scent she'd taken on in Paris, by Chanel she'd said, after I'd asked her about it, a scent she treated herself to on her book tour. A green smell, a little bitter actually, just enough bitter to be something oddly like sweet, which was how her personality turned out finally to be. Till the bitter seemed to prevail.

But after those years of ours together and then my long separation from the touch I'd committedly known, my left hand was holding hers and my right hand was low on her back.

I drew her nearer to me and we danced, just the way we were. She was wearing something now that smelled like fruit, a citrus fruit of an unknown sort, as if it did not exist but on her.

That is how I render these things now. But it was how song and touch and smell worked upon me at our daughter's wedding, worked upon my body, and yes I was quite aware of the part of my body that has no mediating word for a tale like this, a part without an identifying word that is neither clinical nor crude, but I was aware that this cen-

241

tral part of my body was yearning toward her, and it was doing so on its own terms. Neither rational nor wanton.

And after we danced, we thanked each other and we danced once more, and I was actually feeling oddly sweet, but just sweet enough to be feeling something bitter. Then the next song was not suitable for dancing with our mutual dancing skills. We thanked each other, and neither of us could figure out a way to do much else at that moment.

So we went off separately, with a sincere little hug, to mingle and drift and observe.

And meditate. For yes, having yearned for her as I'd held her, I considered Amanda as we once were to each other. As did she, apparently. When the open bar began to close and the lingering few dozen of the hundred guests began to disperse from the library—the newly married couple having disappeared some time ago— Amanda and I found ourselves beside each other as we descended the McKim staircase, and she said, "From a distance tonight I saw a look in you that I'd seen at any number of faculty parties. Even from a distance, I always knew when you'd left the room."

"Tonight, though, only after our newlyweds had gone," I said.

"I noted that too," she said. "You watched them ..." And she paused for a word that seemed to resist her.

We reached the bottom of the staircase and paused.
I looked at her.

She felt the look and met it. "... sweetly," she concluded. And then she embraced the thought by repeating it: "You watched them sweetly."

"But then I left the room, you say."

"I think so."

"Merely to contemplate the occasion we'd had to dance, you and I."

"Ah yes," she said.

Did I stir in that part of me again now?

I must have begun to. For I knew to take her hand.

I thought to say something. I did not know what. So I thought to let her go.

But she lifted our joined hands.

I let her.

She looked at them.

And I said, "What are you thinking?"

She looked me hard in the eyes. And she said, "I'm not *thinking* a thing, you fool." But oh how sweetly she spoke this. Even *fool* was a caress.

In her room down the hall at the Marriott we closed the shades tight, blocking the midsummer twilight.

We knew to trust touch more than sight at this moment.

And touch we did.

After which, fool that I perhaps was—fool that I perhaps am—I had several thoughts:

Metaphorically speaking, how like the hooded Saint Joseph of Arimathea grasping at the Holy Grail with the face of a house cat had been my inciting erection on this day.

And how unexamined—undistracted—the now consummated event itself had felt for me, quite focused as I'd been on my body's readiness, which had thankfully been achieved for the second time on this day—just when it was actionably most relevant—and then focused as I'd been on the nurturing of it into the fundamentals of physical love, an experience quite different from the thrash and dash and improvisation of forty-some years ago, during our first time, in our room in Paris.

And I thought fleetingly how odd it was, following our consummation and my being propped upward upon my pillow against our headboard, that I was moved to light a cigarette. As if from a noirish Fifties film script. Though I had no cigarette to light and, indeed, had not smoked in years nor had ever done so more than intermittently.

And I thought now about how all this was *thinking* indeed, confirming, under the circumstances, Amanda's assessment of me as some sort of fool.

So I turned to her in the dark.

"That was very nice," I said. Unmeditated upon.

ॐ

At this conclusion of Howard's tale, Amanda's shoulders dip a little as she utters a barely audible "Humph," though with the isn't-that-interesting intonation.

She even says aloud, "Interesting."

"Am I correct to hear no disapproval in your *humph*?" Howard asks.

"You are," Amanda says. "The ultimate intervention of your thoughts notwithstanding."

"Which," he says, "I properly recognized …"

"… as perhaps foolish," she says. "Yes. Which helped, though you tried to eat your cake and analyze it too."

Howard shrugs.

"Sorry," she says. "I don't mean to stray from my expression of approval. Indeed, I myself remember your concluding words in the bed as 'That was *lovely*.'"

"Really?"

"Yes."

"The memory not transformed by your writer's unconscious?"

"I'd expect that process in me to have gone the other direction, wouldn't you? To turn your *lovely* into *nice*?"

"That's lovely of you to admit," he says.

"My humph also finds it interesting how our two tales dovetail."

Howard nods in the direction of Amanda's laptop. "Then please read on."

❧

THE SIXTEENTH TALE
Amanda

To be honest, though I'd long been struck by Howard's unwavering approval of our daughter's life choices, culminated in Boston by his unstinting embrace of her partner, and though I was certainly intrigued by his unexpectedly manifest physical desire for me, and though I found myself, at age sixty-two, physically indifferent to all my otherwise available alternate choices of men, even while being capable of my own manifest horniness, I expected sex with my ex-husband to be rather like the haptic incoming-call alert on my mobile phone.

But when he and I were finished and Howard said, "That was lovely," I could only agree.

"Yes," I said. And again: "Yes."

"The possibility of this," he said, "occurred to me even as we danced in the library."

At this point, he had rolled off me—quite gently—and

we lay beside each other on our backs ...

Amanda lifts her face from her laptop to Howard. "I am now breaking off the reading of a sentence where I subsequently made a revision. Consider this next passage a footnote. And I call it that unsarcastically. At this moment I sincerely embrace the form. An interlineary footnote, say."

With an inverted smile Howard nods an approving, how-about-that nod.

She reads on.

As I revisit all this by writing a pandemic tale in a Paris apartment a decade later, I once again have become aware of my frequent differences with Howard over the way we engage with the world, the way we experience even each other, and so I just now reworked this sentence, specifically at this point, based on what has struck me as a revelation, a surprising one this deep into our second marriage. I find myself perceiving a limitation in my own writerly, non-analytical engagement with the world. Which leads me back to admitting how I initially completed this sentence: "... we lay beside each other on our backs, like a couple of dead bodies." Completed it at a remove. Distortingly. As distorted perhaps, in its own way, as if I were trying to create by ratiocination. For it had, in fact, been downright lovely, our having sex together. Without speaking, Howard filled me quite thoroughly. He moved tenderly before moving ardently and then finishing tenderly again, the rhythm of which he himself chose. And afterward, he was gentle even in putting himself beside me where we lay. At the time, I responded to this simply, directly, convincingly. But in the retelling I have abruptly realized that I am capable of being wrongheaded in a manner not so different from his. I use the word advisedly. It was wrong-headed for me to have perpetrated that particular dead-body metaphor. Sense-based though it was, it was willed and thus fraught with thought. My mind once again might have had it that our bodies are unrevivably disconnected. But in the time of my tale, my senses—the very senses I trust as a writer—clearly knew otherwise.

She pauses once more and notes to her scholar of a husband: "End of footnote."

"So noted," he says.

She says, "I shall resume reading from the beginning of the rewritten and footnoted sentence."

Which she does.

At this point, he had rolled off me—quite gently—and we lay beside each other on our backs with our shoulders, our arms, our hands touching. And in that part of me where we were no longer touching, there was a quite noticeable afterglow.

We were silent for a time.

Then Howard turned onto his side, facing me. And he himself acknowledged the word I have now lately flashed on to commit the flawed metaphor. "I misrepresented myself," he said. "The connotation of thoughtfulness is too strong in the word *occurred*. Especially coming from me, with our history together. The possibility of our ending up in bed did not *occur* to me as we danced. I *felt* it."

This I knew to be true.

But I did not mention the proof, though it had certainly invited me to, had opened me to this darkened room. Did not mention it directly. I did, however, let his semantic mea culpa—which surprisingly struck me as endearing—carry me now to another moment with Howard. A moment I had not thought of in a long while.

"I'm reminded," I began to him, as he remained turned on his side there in the bed, all but lying upon me.

I did not immediately finish the sentence.

"Yes?" he asked.

"Do you remember the Temple de la Sybille on the rise in the Buttes-Chaumont?"

"Of course," he said. "Where we met."

"Where we met," I said. "And where we first kissed."

He was silent for a moment. This he seemed not to remember. But it was suddenly clear in me.

"Is that true?"

"That we kissed at our meeting?"

"Yes."

"We did," I said. "Near the very end. Of that I am sure. For I knew that you felt the import of the kiss. The embrace was full-bodied. Involving all the appropriate parts."

He cleared his throat.

Without phlegmy necessity, it seemed to me. With a reflex of anxious discomfort.

He even eased himself down once more upon his back, where he said, "Are you sure this isn't a self-convincing moment from your creative compost?"

"I'm sure," I said.

And to his credit he took my hand in his.

❧❧❧

Amanda sits for a long moment staring at this final sentence. As if, indeed, she were still lying next to her ex-husband-Howard in a bed in Boston and resisting any reflection on his having taken her hand, simply feeling, instead, their two hands clasping.

Howard sits before her, waiting for her eyes to rise to him. But he still holds hands with her a decade ago in a bed in Boston in the sensually manifested way that literature is capable of inducing. And that he is capable of experiencing as a reader no matter what part of his brain is even now gathering itself to intervene.

Though before that intervention comes upon him—indeed, because of his expectation of it—he rises and he steps through the open French doors and onto their balcony and he leans into the railing.

He tries to summon an image of that first kiss on the rocky rise invisible in the park before him, closed by Covid and with only a scattering of post lights.

No actual image comes to him.

But as thoughts go, he thinks, *kissing a beautiful lit-smart coed within an hour of your first meeting in Paris and she noticing your consequent hard-on and remembering it half a century later is a pretty good one.*

At which moment she appears beside him on the balcony.

Their shoulders, their arms, and now even the little-finger edge of their adjacent hands touch.

"So here we are," he says.

"Three weeks later," she says.

"Yes," he says. And after a moment: "I stepped out here because I wanted to remember the kiss."

She does not comment on this at once. The things that come first to her mind are about memory. His sort. Hers. The differences. But it's three weeks later, after all.

Instead, she says, "That's a good sign …"

"Of course I wanted to."

"Enough that you should look into the dark to remember."

"I've been listening to you."

"And did you remember?"

"No," he says. "But I expected the darkness might actually be helpful. If I could not see Sybille's temple, I would have to imagine it."

"Good," she says.

She looks away from him. Into that very dark.

They each have the same thought about what is presently invisible before them: *That was long long ago.*

She lifts her hand and places it on his.

They stand together this way unmoving for a time.

Each of them once again feels small. As when they walked in the plague-silent streets of Paris.

However, it is clear to them both: *The scale may be small. But they stand here inescapably present in their bodies, in the moment.*

Amanda says silently to herself, *There is solace in trying to comprehend that.*

And Howard says to himself, *Ideas are the lie that we can hold back the darkness.*

He turns his hand upward beneath hers.

Their palms press together.

But gently. Mindful of what each knows to be the other's arthritis.

And then without a word, understanding their shared intent, they go inside, to her bed, to touch and to be touched until they sleep.